But Nellie Was So Nice

By Mary McMullen

But Nellie Was So Nice

MARY McMULLEN

DOUBLEDAY & COMPANY, INC.

GARDEN CITY, NEW YORK

All of the characters in this book are fictitious, and any resemblance to actual persons, living or dead, is purely coincidental.

To Peggy and Bill

But Nellie Was So Nice

Part One

One

After a grim winter and a malicious March, the morning in early April, soft and yellow as buttercups, didn't deserve the dark hang of doom about it.

The darkness. What was it?

Nellie Hand usually awakened on all cylinders, but her mind now allowed her a half-minute of blankness.

Seven o'clock sunlight making a clean blaze of the blue and white cafe curtains on the windows across from the bed. The nice feel of sheets put on fresh yesterday, but wildly rumpled, she noticed, as though she'd been tossing in a nightmare.

"Nellie? I know it's late, I just had to call you—"

It began to come back in its entirety, word by word.

Don't think about the telephone call—something she might have dreamed, except of course she hadn't—at least until after breakfast. It couldn't be handled while she lay here, defenseless and stricken. One is so helpless on one's back.

Two o'clock in the morning, it had started, then gone on for twenty-five minutes or so. But of course there had been long pauses between the words, and her own efforts to cut it off, dam the stream.

". . . I don't think you should be telling me this . . . you're probably just overtired . . . now honestly, Matthew, how many brandies have you had? . . . Matthew. Stop."

Over the past several years, she had gotten used to the small-hours calls from Matthew Jones, Executive Vice President, Sales, United Broadcasting Company. Not given to flattering herself, she put it down to the fact that once or twice a month he just couldn't sleep.

She had met him at a party, right downstairs, at Ursula's. A big tall jovial substantially built man in his forties, with a broad pink face and very black hair and eyebrows and beautiful clothes. A dark blue English-tailored suit, white shirt polka-dotted in currant red, richly knotted navy and red striped tie. Exuding success, money, charm, and Uptown—not at all a Greenwich Village type.

He had noticed on being introduced to her that her glass was empty and courteously took it away to refill it, then had fallen into conversation with her about the weather, and the Middle East, and football. Of the three subjects, the only one that interested her was the weather. But she was by nature as well as long practice a good listener, comfortable, absorbed-looking, responsive. When he and his wife Joy left, he said in her ear, "I like you, Nellie Hand. We're going to be friends. Aren't we?"

It was quite innocent as far as Nellie was concerned. Nothing for Joy to worry about even if she was aware of the late-night calls, which perhaps she wasn't. He seemed always to be stretched out on the suede sofa in his library when he called her.

Odd that you could reach the age of fifty-three before discovering that glisteningly successful people could have their moments of being lonely, of being lost.

He would talk to her about his boyhood memories—a dog he'd loved, the wrench when they'd had to give up the big house in Bronxville after his father had committed suicide and there turned out to be no money at all, nothing but bills.

"And you know, Nellie dear, like father like son, I'm up to here in debt, can't seem to cure myself of it."

He would read her poems of Dylan Thomas he liked, and once, shyly, he read her a poem of his own. It was a terrible poem but she responded with warm kind attention. "I do like that last line, I won't forget it easily."

He would discuss books he was reading, proudly announce new accounts he had landed. It was always about him and never about her but she didn't mind. It was in a way flattering, she supposed. His night companion, his relied-upon ear.

"You have no life of your own," Lise Kozer scolded. "You're at everybody's service."

But last night, or this morning, he had talked about—

Move. Get up.

Yes, don't think about it. Or certainly not until she'd had some coffee. For the moment, draw a veil, as her mother used to say.

There was a deep growl from the living room and the snarl of a cat. "Now then, let's be chums!" Nellie called, startling herself by the sound of her own voice. She was keeping the great dark golden afghan, Titania, for her friend Josephine Gray until next Tuesday.

Friends found it much more convenient to leave their pets with good-natured Nellie than to go to the expense of boarding them out; besides, animals were so much happier and more contented in a *home* atmosphere.

Her handsome tiger cat George took a lightning swipe at the afghan's nose and then shot into the bathroom and up onto the washbasin, where he stayed while she showered. She had a strong belief in the efficacy of the morning shower. Wash away worry, wash away yesterday, soap and scrub, start today all new, brand new. April was too early but beginning along about May she would finish off with a one-minute breath-catching douse of cold water.

". . . the police never had a hint, a—excuse the expression—a clue. I suppose in an academic sense the case is still open on their books, but with all they have on their plates day to day . . ."

Turn the voice down and off. Putting your head in the sand may be foolishness, but sometimes a wise sort of foolishness. Go from motion to motion, give each your full attention. Make coffee, and while it drips make toast. Let's see, there's a fresh peach to eat with the toast, from that beautiful great basket in Jane Follins' room at St. Vincent's Hospital.

The telephone rang while she was dressing. She was a saleswoman at Babylon on University Place and most of her clothes were Enid Callender's mistakes, spectacularly marked down, and then with her 30 per cent discount quite good buys. Perhaps rather a strong purple, and the ruffle at the hem might be a bit young for her, but April was the time for high hearts and bright colors.

"Nellie?" Lise's deep thick heavily accented voice. She was half Dutch and half Greek, and Nellie had never been able to decide which nationality spoke. "I have had, let me tell you, the most terrible night." The details of her night took several minutes, and then she came to her other point. "I must, I must have a bowl of your heavenly cabbage soup this evening," and then as an obvious afterthought, "and of course your delightful company."

Good. Something else to fasten her mind on. Would she have time to come home at noon and make the soup? It tasted much better after it had sat awhile in the refrigerator; the poultry seasoning had time to penetrate the onions and potatoes.

She leashed the afghan. "Must empty you out," she informed her. Her apartment was a fourth-floor walk-up; she had lived in it for twenty years and could have managed the stairs blindfolded.

Passing Ursula Winter's door on the third floor, she thought how nice it would be to discuss it with Ursula. Have it brushed away as a tale told after midnight, brought on by brandy, a fancy, a self-dramatization—Ursula after all knew Matthew.

But honor forbade her discussing it with anyone. Ever.

Except possibly, in a pinch, a really desperate pinch, with her nephew Jeremy.

Titania's excretion, if large, was neat. Nellie scooped it with her sand shovel into her sand pail. She walked in the early warm sunlight to the end of Timothy Street, which ran for only two blocks, and back along the other side. Her building, narrow, tall, shabby yellow stucco, was on the corner.

On the ground floor front, two steps went up on one side to a blue door that needed a new coat of paint. To the right was the large plate-glass display window of the Ditto Gallery. The window this morning held a lighted transparency of Gainsborough's "The Blue Boy." Beside it on an easel was a superbly accurate copy in oils, ornately gilt-framed.

The gallery's artist-in-residence and proprietor, Basil Perov, was hosing his sidewalk in a European manner. He was a short, square-chested, lusty man with sparkling brown eyes under thorny heavy brows, a high hard shining forehead from which the crinkled red-brown hair was retreating, taut rosy cheeks, and a full-lipped sensual mouth with a little raised frill of flesh edging it.

"Good morning, queen of the fourth-floor back!" he shouted. She was no more than six feet away from him but she was sure he could be heard as far as Christopher Street. His stentorian voice had deliberately kept its Russian roll. "Mind the spray, we do not wish to shower your fetching purple garrrb."

He wore a sort of Village uniform—corduroys and a turtle-necked dark jersey and leather sandals—but he didn't look like anybody else. In spite of his lack of height, he had a princely stride, and gave an impression of a good deal of muscle and bone. Nellie had always found him a merry man and was devoted to him.

He turned off the hose and lit a cigarette. "If it wasn't so early I'd offer you vodka. You look a little, is it peaky? Did I hear you on the telephone in the small hours?"

At her startled look, he said, "Lenin was shrieking his head off on your fire-escape landing and I finally gave up and went and got him. I suppose he wanted to quarrel with George. I heard your voice—either talking in your sleep or on the phone. Nellie! At after 2 A.M.! Have you taken a lover?"

Good God, what on her end had she said, what could he have overheard? "I don't think you should be telling me this" and how many other giveaway tag ends?

Over an unnerving flurry of heartbeats, she said, "Someone— I don't think you know her—who couldn't sleep." A woman friend named Matthew?

He was looking at her in a penetrating way, but that was his natural manner, she reminded herself. Artists probably developed the habit of using their eyes in a hundred per cent sort of fashion.

"Too bad, a lover would have been a much more rewarding interruption to your dreams. I will *not* say have a good day but my fondest wishes and regards follow you across town to Babylon."

The four-story climb as a rule didn't tire her, she was so used to it. But this morning she rested for a moment at the top before unlocking her door. Her knees felt odd.

Turn off your mind, you'll never get through the day this way. She put on a light skim of makeup, remembered to take her vitamin pill, filled Titania's water bowl, gave jealous George an extra stroking, and left the apartment gratefully.

On the way to work, she lifted a hand and called an almost cheerful hello to a dozen people. She paused for a moment in front of a sidewalk stand of spring flowers on Eighth Street. Such a seething street by night, such a bright bustling neighborhood street by day. Too early yet for the tourists; people doing normal things, eating breakfast behind glass, marketing.

Daffodils, ninety-nine cents a bunch. Perhaps on the way home at noon to make the soup . . . The buds were plump, green-yellow, and tight; they were admirable daffodils. On her birthday, in February, Matthew had sent her an immense long box layered with daffodils, narcissus, and freesia. To my dear pal Nell, many happy returns, M.

What was he thinking, feeling, this morning, remembering what he had told her? Push it away. Back to the sand again. She had a living to make. She knew she had a reputation for absent-mindedness (it amused her friends) but the next step was to turn scatty, and this must be avoided at all costs.

". . . did you see Nellie bustling along to Babylon? Didn't she look *weird?*"

Faces could betray secrets. Keep your face open. And calm.

She was glad it turned out to be a minute-to-minute busy day right from the unlocking of the door of Enid Callender's boutique.

Babylon was a long-established and popular shop, crammed untidily and fascinatingly full of colorful and tempting clothes, separates, at-home things, accessories, and costume jewelry. It occupied a floor space of twenty by forty feet. Behind were Enid's tiny office and two dressing booths curtained in apple-green canvas. The carpet was a battered but clean Persian, dim cream and jade. There was a crisp fresh smell of lavender from Enid's pomander balls hanging from the rose-painted mirrored ceiling. The decor had no rhyme or reason. But it was somehow a desirable place to be in.

An occasional tourist in search of baby clothes turned away baffled and resentful when Babylon proved to have none in stock.

The telephone started ringing in Enid's office the moment Nellie closed the street door behind her. Enid's own voice, deep, aristocratic: "Nellie? I won't be in until sometime this afternoon, I was sighting a UFO, I swear it was one, and I fell over a heap of garbage cans. I must hobble to the doctor, my ankle—thank God they were empty. The cans, I mean."

Peculiar accidents and adventures were always happening to
Enid, and Nellie was in no way startled, but she murmured her
sympathy.

Enid had been everywhere, done everything in her sixty hec-
tic years; it would be nice if she could pour it all out to Enid,
who was completely unshockable.

He hadn't even told her not to tell anyone else. But of course
he would have thought there was no need to: the stricture was
implicit in his story, his terrible story.

What was Enid saying? "—If that naughty Lukie is late again,
give her a good sound scolding."

That naughty Lukie was Lucinda Callender, Enid's niece. She
worked two days a week at Babylon. "For pot money, I suppose,"
was Enid's opinion, "if not worse. But, except for the hair, and
the clothes, she does look like my sweet sister Millicent. If I
wasn't an atheist I'd say rest her soul, well, rest it anyway."

Enid's SPRING SALE sign in the window drew a buzz of customers. Lukie came in at eleven, an hour late, and for a moment
Nellie stared at her in confusion, wondering who this was—surely
someone she knew?

To her customer, she said, "Yes, we have it in orange, but the
orange isn't marked down, would you like to try it on anyway?"

The long hazel-blond hair had been decoratively and carelessly slashed to nape length and dyed Titian red. The perfect
skin, usually whistle-bare of makeup, wore a coating of unlikely
creamy peach, the mouth was scarlet, the brows tweezed to an
almost invisible line under the big dark purple goggles. She still
wore the everlasting jeans, but the white blouse was wildly ruffled, and tangled in the ruffles were four or five necklaces. Brace-
lets all up one arm clanked and crashed gently.

She looks like a tart, Nellie thought, instead of a health-food
ad as she usually does. Not one to withhold her curiosity and
look the other way, she said, "The orange is thirty-nine fifty . . .
what on earth, Lukie?"

A brief scarlet-and-white grin. "Just hiding from someone I
heard might be coming downtown looking for me. Would you
mind calling me Lucinda for a week or so? Or better still what
they called me at school, Lulu."

"Is he apt to come here?" Nellie asked a little apprehensively.

It never occurred to her that the someone could be other than a male.

"He doesn't know where I work. I think we're safe. For the time being."

"You take over for a bit," Nellie said. "I'm going into the office to make myself some coffee, and sit down."

Two

"Nellie? I know it's late, I just had to call you."

Soup or no soup, it had been a mistake to come back to the apartment at noon.

An unseen tape began to play.

Let's see, four potatoes and four onions and four cups of chopped cabbage should make enough for at least three bowls for Lise.

A useless attempt to concentrate on other things, dismiss the voice on the tape.

"There's something I have to tell you. You're the only one in the world I could tell, and you know I trust you absolutely. I can't carry it around by myself any longer, Nellie, I can't stand it. Maybe if I tell you—let some air into my dark closet—I can stand living with it better. Because I will have to, the rest of my life."

Marital infidelity? she had wondered at the time. Some kind of business wrongdoing? And he coming to her as a Catholic to the confessional? Of course she could listen to him, but she would have no absolution to offer him except her attention and her sympathy.

"It happened tonight, five years ago tonight, which is why I suppose I . . . but you have to understand all the things that happened before, that led up to it."

His autobiography again, from young boyhood on, most of which she knew. His father's suicide, the crash into poverty, into want. Working his way through college and in the middle of that his mother's death of a heart attack—"but at her age, having to go to work at Macy's, standing on her feet all day, dollars and cents, or the lack of them, is what really killed her."

After graduation, all the jobs that hadn't worked out; he had wanted success too desperately, too quickly. Advertising. Sales promotion. Public relations. A stint as advertising manager with an obscure mattress company in Albany. Managing, briefly, a liquor store, where he said he had really learned to drink hard. Then finding his feet, out of town and for the moment far away from competition, in radio.

"TV of course was the big thing so radio wasn't so hard to get into, particularly if you had the voice, and you know my purple velvet baritone, Nellie . . ."

Disc jockey at small stations, Jacksonville, Bridgeport, Burbank, Seattle, Denver, with each progression a little more money until he was doing what other men would consider quite well.

He had moved up to station manager in Denver. "I did something stupid there. I was up to my ass in debt, had to dress the part you know, had to live in the right place and entertain the right people, so I helped myself to fifty thousand dollars from the till. It was a bad time for me, I was in love with a woman, she was married, no go. I didn't know what I was doing from hour to hour. They caught me and I went to jail for two years. Jail, Nellie. Me."

"I don't think you should be telling me this," she had said. "You're probably overtired—"

"But this is only the beginning. This is only the reason *why*, Nellie."

"But still do you think you should . . . ?"

"I have to. I must." A pause: what sounded like a gulp of drink going down. "When I got out I changed my name, took my own middle one and my mother's maiden name, and started all over again, out in the boondocks. But of course I knew all the ropes and they thought, This Matthew Jones is really on the ball, there's nothing he doesn't know about radio."

Up the ladder again, much faster, and then the plum dropped into his hands, the job with United Broadcasting in New York. Up United's ladder; in two years, he was a sales vice president. Internal politics, a head rolling, made the job of executive vice president open overnight. Two men were in the running, pretty well neck and neck, Matthew and Roy Cox.

Peel the parboiled potatoes, add the onions, simmer in not much water.

And stop right here before it's too late.

The voice wouldn't stop.

"Cox had a beach place on Long Island. He told me he was going out there, one weekend in early April, to start to get the place fixed up. He said why didn't I join him for a bachelor night out, Saturday, leave Joy home. I thought he had some kind of deal in mind, maybe he'd back off and leave the field to me, maybe he wanted money. I went."

Her heart was beating hard. Voice sounding a little winded, she said, "Hang on a minute, the dog's water bowl is empty and he's banging it around on the floor, to wake the . . ." For some reason she didn't add the last word.

She went and got herself two fingers of scotch and considered just hanging up the telephone. Maybe he'd think something had gone wrong with the connection.

But she picked up the receiver. "Yes? . . . You went to have a night out—"

"The son of a bitch poured me a drink and then said, 'Let's get down to business.' It was about nine o'clock. He got out a manila folder, a dossier on Matthew Jones-Roger Lloyd. It turned out he'd been working in Denver when I was, peddling advertising space for a local newspaper. He remembered my voice. Didn't say anything about it, about me, until it looked as though it could come in real handy for him. He had it all down. The sum involved, the dates, the jail sentence, the name change. I still thought—if at the time I could think at all—that he wanted money. But he didn't. Just for me to back down, that's what he wanted, hand over the running to him. Do you know what happens when you're passed over in this business, Nellie? You've not only missed out on a particular job, you've lost the race, you've had it. You're the man who almost made it but didn't so therefore never will. Flush Matthew Jones, flush him at United and CBS and NBC and ABC."

The racing voice terrified her. "Matthew. Stop."

With a sort of gentle surprise, "It's too late now to stop, isn't it. Well then. You know, or maybe you don't, that about once a year I let my terrible temper go, the rest of the time I send it down to curdle my ulcer. I went for him. I got his neck in my hands. Everything was buzzing. Everything was red. I pressed, and I pressed, and when I let go he fell over my feet. He stayed there. He was dead. I killed him."

Into her silence he repeated, "I killed him, Nellie, did you hear me? I choked him to death with my hands. I murdered him. I finished him." Patiently spacing and emphasizing each syllable, forever damning, "I . . . *killed* . . . him."

Now, seeming unable to wait for any response from her, he went on with a change of voice, eager, plaintive, "But you do see there's nothing else I could have done? You do see that, Nellie? It was my whole life that was at stake, mine against his. If I did back down, *I* was finished. If I didn't, I was even more finished, down an even bigger blacker hole, crook, jailbird, the suave Matthew Jones . . . I mean, I think under the circumstances, any man would . . ."

He paused as though waiting for an assent she couldn't give. She tried to finish her scotch and choked on it.

"Consider your back thumped," he said. "Go ahead, get your breath back. Well anyway, Nellie, the police never had a hint, a —excuse the expression—a clue."

Roy Cox had ended up as a brief third-page story in the *Times*. Television executive found murdered in his beach house near Sag Harbor. As it was off-season, the straggle of cottages along Merganser Beach were almost empty. There had been vandalism, robberies at the next beach down, Tibbets'. Police hazarded a guess that Cox, coming out for the weekend, had surprised a burglar and been killed in the struggle. He was a man alone, divorced, no children. And he obviously would have told no one about his plan to blackmail Matthew Jones out of the executive vice presidency by means of a sheet of white bond paper.

Two weeks later, in the advertising column of the *Times*, Matthew's promotion was announced.

"I suppose in an academic sense the case is still open on their books, but with all they have on their plates day to day . . . Yes, I don't see what else I could have done. By God I don't. In a strange way I feel better about it. I think I can sleep, in a little while. Thank Christ for the only ear in the world that could ever hear all of this." Voice low, rasping. "But I've talked my throat sore. I'm off to the Coast tomorrow for a week, I'll call you when I get back. Bless you, Nellie. We can both sleep now."

Three

Go home at six, when Babylon closed, except for Thursdays and Saturdays, when it was open until ten. Climb the stairs, take Titania out, go back up again, put the soup in her large teakettle, feed George and the afghan, down the stairs again and over to Eighth Street where Lise Kozer lived, halfway up the block between Fifth and Sixth.

"In-again-out-again-Finnegan," Nellie said aloud; but she was glad of the necessary bustle. Since noon, her mind had been deliberately screening out everything but the immediate visible and audible realities.

A man passing by heard her and studied her and her battered teakettle with interest. She was a short, plump woman with a lift and doughtiness to her carriage, her walk. She had a dimply round face with a daintily pointed chin, a young voice, high and soft, and curiously young blue eyes under sandy brows and lashes. Her graying red hair, more than ready for her next haphazard dye job, was cut short and tumbled in bangs over her forehead. She had spilled some of her four o'clock coffee on her dress—"I'm a great spiller," she had commented ruefully to three customers—and had changed into a Roman-striped caftan which came down to the heels of her sturdy, sensible, brown T-strap pumps. She had very little vanity, and didn't mind looking a bit peculiar, as she knew she did this evening; the great thing was to be comfortable.

Eighth Street was tuning up for the hours after dark. She was jostled at the corner by a band of tough-looking girls dressed alike in black vinyl nail-headed jackets and tight black jeans, by costume and demeanor loudly proclaiming themselves lesbians.

"Nell, dear lady!" The young man known locally as Mr. Clean fell into step beside her for a few yards. He was shaved bald and dressed in white muslin Indian garments, a tunic and calf-gripping trousers. It was generally understood that he was the scion of a Cleveland cereal empire and was paid sixty thousand dollars a year to stay away from home. But perfectly harmless, people said. He was now, as almost always, gently and tidily drunk. "Are you offering tea to the multitudes? It would be like your kind heart to do so."

"No, it's soup," Nellie said, and Mr. Clean without a word of farewell abruptly crossed the street.

Two young men walked toward her, both with string shopping bags, each clasping the hand of a small girl between them. Obviously, in one way or another, they were her parents.

The starers on the sidewalks just about equaled the number of the stared-at. Prostitutes, Nellie thought, passing a silver-blonde she knew by sight and nodded to, were in a way so comfortably old-*fashioned*. Rock snarled and roared from a record shop and the smell of hot oily popcorn assailed her small tilted nose. She was long since used to the no-bra business—"Nippling around town," Jeremy called it—but she did think that that skirt slit to the waist in front, nothing but black lace bikini pants under it, was a little— And with the sun down it wasn't all that warm, the girl might easily take a chill.

The woman familiar to the neighborhood as the Lady in Red drifted toward her. She was always dressed head to foot in the one color: tonight, great droop-brimmed red felt hat, red fake fur jacket, billowing red chiffon skirt, red tights around wizened ankles, red high-heeled sandals. She would continue her drift until she reached Rick's, on Sheridan Square, where she could be seen sitting at the bar consuming her nightly three Pernods before drifting out again. Nellie often wondered to what long-ago romance the blazing color was a memorial; she must be well over seventy.

The two exchanged quick ducking nods. "Lovely evening, but I think coming on for rain," said the Lady in Red, not exactly to Nellie, but shyly, to the air in front of her. Her voice was old and cracked. She didn't wait for a response.

Perhaps not a romance, but a tragedy. Red for blood. For violent death. *Death.*

"*I killed him.*" Her traitorous mind snatched her off Eighth

Street and back onto the telephone. A hole seemed to yawn open
in the universe and she felt about to fall into it. She tripped over
the hem of her caftan and a hand reached out to catch her, steady
her. Through a dark haze she saw a thin young man in black
ballet tights and jersey. "Are you all right?" "Yes . . . thank you
so much . . ." A deep breath or two ought to help. But don't lean
against the tempting wall or people will think you're recovering
from too many drinks. Lise was just next door.

Her apartment was over a seafood restaurant. Too bad even
the best fish smell like *fish* when they're cooking, Nellie made
herself muse as she climbed the long flight of stairs.

At her knock, a voice called, "Come in, I've just unlocked the
door for you," and then when she opened the door, Lise gazed in
extravagant surprise and delight. "Nellie! It's you! And the soup
too, in that so beautiful container. You've made my evening for
me!"

She was lying on her shabby, soiled, old green sofa with a
faded quilt over her legs. She had been an on-and-off invalid for
all the years Nellie had known her; her condition had finally re-
solved itself into, or been belatedly diagnosed as, leukemia.
Nellie had fallen into the habit of seeing to her needs when she
had the time. In spite of her oddities and her demands, Lise was
regarded by her as an old and valued friend.

She shook off the depression that always hit her when she arrived here. The death sentence hanging in the air. And long before it had been pronounced, the bottom-of-the-well atmosphere
of the apartment. Dark, drab, never more than one lamp lit,
shades pulled behind heavy dusty curtains to the windowsills.
You never knew when you were at Lise's whether it was day or
night outside. There were no comforts, no color, no gaiety, nothing at all female.

Lise, still ambulatory when she felt like it, got off the sofa and
followed her into the grim little kitchen, watching as she poured
some of the soup from the teakettle into a chipped white enameled pot. She sniffed hungrily.

"Ah, the scent, the fragrance. For this, Nellie, you shall have,
when my money comes through, a set of Sèvres, a full set, your
own dinnerware is a disgrace."

When the litigation in Holland was over. When her money

came through. For this, you shall have, dear Nellie, a mink coat, not common brown but black or a pale pale silver . . . a pair of diamond earrings, nothing does so much for a woman's face . . . two weeks in Paris at the Bristol.

Nellie wasn't sure the money wasn't a fantasy. But Lise had been consistent and vociferous about it for a matter of eight years. Her father, she said, had been a diamond merchant in Amsterdam, a man of immense wealth. It was his arrangement with his partner, and the lawsuits and squabbles of the partner's children and nephews and nieces, that had tied up her rightful inheritance, she said. The lawyer representing Lise and her sister Gretel in Amsterdam had written, according to her New York lawyer, that a breakthrough was in sight in two, three, four months.

She lived, while waiting for her flood of gold, on a small fixed income from her mother's estate.

"But the richest woman in New York, Nellie, couldn't eat finer soup," she said, back on her sofa again, spooning the soup greedily. Nellie had pulled up a table, found a wrinkled paper napkin for a place mat, sliced fresh rye bread and buttered it.

"Ahhhh . . ." Lise finished her soup. "If you weren't here I'd lick the plate. Now you will if you please get me a large drink of the Jack Daniels, no ice, no water, and have one yourself. I have something to tell you."

She lay back, sipping her drink, brooding. A big woman, with hooded dark eyes, purple stains underneath them, coarse sallow skin, wildly curly short dark gray hair, a thick-lipped mouth that was strong, sardonic, and sometimes bitter in its curves. My age roughly, Nellie had decided, although Lise never mentioned it: say fifty-five or so.

"I wrote a letter this afternoon to that beast. That monster." Nellie had no need to ask to whom she was referring. That beast was her sister Gretel.

"I told her—please pass me my cigarettes—that you are to be my heir, that she is to be cut off without a penny, a penny of mine at least. As the older sister, and as Papa's favorite, I am to get two-thirds. If there's anything left, that is, after those bloody lawyers finish their fight to the death."

Nellie made the small demurring distressed sounds she always

made when Lise obliquely referred to her death and her naming
Nellie as her beneficiary.

"Rather than let *her* have it, or her pig of a husband, I would
leave it to a camel in the zoo," Lise said, thus relieving her puta-
tive heir of some of the burden of gratitude.

She drank an inch of her Jack Daniels. "Yes, I know I've told
you before, but I want no questions in *anybody's* mind in this
case. It's all taken care of, I had that clod, that nincompoop"—
read by Nellie as her lawyer Charles Lambert, a cousin of Enid's
—"here all morning. And now let us forget such things. I may
have two years, three. Let us be merry. Hand me the bottle."

The telephone on the end table rang. Lise snatched it up, listened, and then scowled. "For you. Charmian."

Charmian Lyle said in her soft vague voice, "I've been phoning
everywhere, don't you remember you said you'd come around
for dinner tonight? Walter's away, and I'm lonely, and your
chicken breast is almost done."

"I'll be over in ten minutes," Nellie promised.

Lise scowled again. "How selfish people are! You on your feet
all day and now you must gallop to her beck and call. But it's
your own fault, Nellie, you should learn how to say no."

"No to chicken breast and probably a glass of champagne? I
must run, there's enough soup for another meal or so. I'll just put
it in the refrigerator."

"Don't forget that family heirloom of yours, the teakettle,"
Lise said jealously. "Vintage Woolworth, is it?"

Descending the staircase, Nellie thought that probably tomorrow morning she would be disinherited.

Later it seemed to her astonishing that it wasn't until she was
walking along quiet West Eleventh Street in the dusk that fear
struck her, suddenly and hard, fear for herself.

It was triggered by a soft footfall close behind her. When she
turned her head, she saw a small boy of six or so. He was wearing yellow and white striped pajamas.

"Oh dear," she said. "Should you be out alone, at this hour,
and in your bed pajamas?"

He opened his hand to show her a lime. "I went next door to
borrow it." He had daffodil yellow hair, gray eyes, and a curly

tender mouth. He took a little skip past her and began to go up the stairs of a brownstone with a white-painted fanlighted door. On the third step up, he turned suddenly back and said, "Guess what."

"What?" Nellie asked, wanting to see him safely in the house.

"My mother's thirty-two." He studied the lime in his hand and then with sparkling interest Nellie's face. "It's her birthday. Everybody's having a drink. Would you like to come in and have a drink?"

"I'd love to, but I have to be somewhere. Do wish her happy birthday for me."

"All right, I will." The little boy paused and turned again at the top of the stairs, his hand on the doorknob. It was as though he wanted to fix something firmly in time, the gaiety inside, the purple dusk, his mother's birthday, the nice woman who worried about his being out on the street in his bed pajamas.

"Will you be passing by tomorrow?" he asked. "Will I see you tomorrow?"

"If not tomorrow, then soon," Nellie said. "I often go by your house."

How ungrateful we are, she thought—or how ungrateful I am —to forget in the daily scuttle how sweet life is. How much when you think about it you want to go on living it.

But Matthew has, to all intents and purposes, put his life and the living of it into my hands.

Up until now, when she allowed herself to think about it, she worried about the story itself. That someone she knew and was very fond of could have killed, extinguished a life between his thumbs. Amiable, jovial, pink Matthew, now with a great invisible black-purple birthmark staining his face. Or did she mean the mark of Cain?

And the burden, the living with it, the going back to just the moment before he reached for a throat . . . *If only I'd stopped then, had another drink, reasoned with him—who knows, it might have been as simple as that.*

He had said, "You know I trust you absolutely."

But what if he began to worry about letting air into his dark closet and handing a deadly secret to someone else, no matter how trustworthy?

She was aware that she might be described as a gossip. (She had never been quite sure where the line lay between being interested in other people and their doings, and being thus labeled.) But only about inconsequential daily things, not big things, dangerous things, things that must be kept quiet. God only knew how many there were of these, for which she had been the repository since she was in her twenties. Promise not to tell anyone, Nellie, but I just have to talk to you about . . .

When she got to Charmian's, should she call and see if he really was out of town, off to the Coast? Try his private line at UBC, in case he was working late, and if he wasn't there call the apartment? About what? If he had been drinking brandy, a lot of it—and you could never tell from his practiced perfect enunciation—he might have forgotten, or half-forgotten, or thought he'd dreamed it. Her voice might be the coin in the slot, bringing it all crisply and immediately back to him.

My God, it happened, now I remember, I did tell her.

And even if Joy answered, and said "Yes, he left this morning for California," how could you be sure that—?

Did, dear God, his wife Joy know about it? Some of it? ". . . thank Christ for the only ear in the world that could ever hear all of this . . ." *All.* The deed itself? Or the rationale leading to it, trying to justify it. "But you do see there's nothing else I could have done?"

Surely it would have been the natural thing for him to call her frantically sometime this morning, from his apartment or the airport.

"Nellie, forget what I told you last night, will you?"

And then something along the lines of: "Of course it never happened at all. A fantasy of mine, and you have no idea of the guilt, wanting to kill a man, wanting to so badly you can taste it. Actually he—Roy Cox—is alive and well and making a fortune at CBS." Or NBC. Or ABC. Or with any company, anywhere in the country. She would never have any way of knowing whether he was or not. Alive.

Maybe Matthew was still airborne. Or, having arrived, was trapped in some coastal conference. Three hours' time difference. Let's see, it's seven ten here, it would only be four ten there. Yes, he'd probably call tonight. He'd certainly call tonight. And she'd say, "But I never did believe it really happened anyway."

And that would be that. Wouldn't it?

Four

Charmian Lyle had given herself her first name at the age of sixteen, upon encountering it in an English novel. Her baptismal name was Ethel. When her husband Walter was extremely angry with her, he called her Ethel.

Charmian, she thought, suited her much better. She didn't think she looked, felt, or sounded like an Ethel. Nor like her middle name, which she really detested, Edna.

She was, then and now at thirty-one, beautiful. Tall and languorous in bone, flesh, and motion. Skin of colorless matte ivory, great gray eyes even softer and more striking because she was myopic and refused to wear glasses and couldn't bear contact lenses. The eyes were deep-set under eggshell Botticelli lids. Her mouth was wide and delicate, her throat line poetically long, her forehead high, cupped, under loosely petaled hair of a natural silver-gilt color, pale as moonlight.

At twenty-six, she had married Walter Lyle. "Well, after all," she would explain, "everyone I knew, boys, I mean, men, were more or less barefoot, and looking a horrible mess, and on things, aren't drugs boring? and refusing to do anything as square as making a living, so what would you have done in my place?" She had grown up in the Village, on West Ninth Street between Fifth and Sixth, and on her marriage flatly refused to move uptown, to the East Sixties or Seventies Walter thought a more appropriate setting for a wife of his.

"But I can't move away from my friends, I'd be absolutely lost."

"There are taxis, and subways, and buses," Walter had pointed out, to no avail. The Village or nowhere, she said. In some matters, her word was law. They first took a brownstone next to the one she had lived in for nineteen years and then moved to their present twelfth-story penthouse in a new, pillared, marble-faced building on West Eleventh Street.

There had never been any idea of her remaining at her job as a model at Bergdorf Goodman, where she could be seen drifting about the main floor or through the designers' salon, or dazzling the company in one of the elevators. The wife of a rising star at Intercoastal Petroleum did not, could not, work for a living.

She had nothing to do from morning till night but amuse herself, which made her rely heavily on her friends, and on armloads of rental library books; fortunately for her, she loved to read.

Walter adored her. The other side of the coin of his obsessive love was jealousy. His chambered nautilus, all silver and gold and gray and ivory—who now, at this or any other minute, was lusting for her? Calling her up? Sending her flowers which of course she would have to have disposed of by the time he got home. Making lunch dates with her in those hidden, secret little Village restaurants where no one would see them.

He called her two or three times a day to make sure she was home, and alone; or if she wasn't, to get an explanation of where she had been.

"Poor darling," Charmian said of him tolerantly. If it was a bit annoying, it was also flattering.

But she almost rebelled when she found out about the tape, which she discovered after it had been running busily five days a week for six months. One night, unable to sleep, she had gotten out of bed and was going to the kitchen for hot milk when, passing Walter's study, she heard her own voice. ". . . yes, I'd love lunch, especially on a rainy day. Enrico and Paglieri's? I could use a big bowl of minestrone . . ."

"But I don't want to miss a minute of you, my darling," Walter explained. "Your voice, your laugh, your doings—I only have you evenings, nights, mornings, and weekends, and life is short. Think how much Charmian I'm missing."

For him, quite a flight, Charmian had thought, touched; Walter was not given to exposing his emotions and usually talked in quiet correct tones of gray.

The machine was in a louvered cabinet in a handsome built-in teak storage wall at one end of the living room. It was kept locked, and only Walter had the key to it. "I don't want you edit-

ing yourself. I mean, if you occasionally lose your temper and
swear, that's fun to listen to, too."

Walter's tape was somewhat of a joke among Charmian's
friends. When Enid came to visit, she always said in a raised
greeting voice, "Hello there, Walter, how are you this fine day?
I'm quite well, thank you."

"He's Boswell to your Johnson," Ursula Winter said. "I hope
you remember to polish your telephone conversations. An apt
quotation here and there makes good listening and tags you as a
person of culture."

She had no idea whether there were extensions of the record-
ing device—bugs?—in the bedroom (the kitchen didn't matter)
and had never had the courage to ask. Walter might read things
into such an inquiry.

Nellie thought that this jealous eavesdropping was indecent
and conceivably dangerous. The suspicious ear could give all
sorts of sinister meanings to even the most innocent of words, of
phrases. She was always, at Charmian's apartment, vaguely uncomfortable.

Walter, now hear this, she said to herself, apologizing for being late. Charmian said, "It's all right, do collapse on the sofa,
you look terribly tired, Nellie. Funny, I've never seen you looking really tired before. Joy Jones called a few minutes ago, she
said she'd been calling you everywhere, trying to reach you, just
like me."

Nellie's heart gave one tremendous thump. "Did she say what
she wanted?"

"No. Would you like to call her?"

"Not right now. Yes, thank you . . . I will have a little champagne." Charmian herself drank nothing but champagne. "I'll
catch up with her later."

Over the chicken breasts, which had been baked in apricots,
shallots and wine, Charmian said, "We're going to be painted in
a few days. May I borrow your apartment during the day to take
refuge? Short of a bomb or an earthquake, being painted is the
most destroying thing I know."

"Yes, of course, if you don't mind the fact that I haven't been
painted for six years."

The telephone rang while Charmian was in the middle of a

bite of avocado filled with sautéed mushrooms. There was an extension phone in the candlelit white dining room but Charmian went into the living room. "Darling!" Nellie heard her say.

Be careful, Charmian, Nellie thought, hearing a drink at the Amen Corner at the Fifth Avenue Hotel being arranged for tomorrow evening. "Walter won't be home until Thursday, Amanda, you have no idea how lonely I am, a petroleum widow . . ."

Coming back to the table, Charmian said, "My cousin Amanda. She's in on a buying trip, she works for Neiman-Marcus, you know. She's only been out there two years but I swear she's gotten herself a Texas accent."

Her eyes were hazily brilliant. There was a sudden soft bloom on her which had nothing to do with the candlelight. Seizing upon the opportunity to think about anything and anybody except her own preoccupation, Nellie wondered who Amanda really was and how deeply he and Charmian were involved. And whether it was just starting or had been going on for some time.

It's a good thing Walter can't see her right this minute. Or maybe she doesn't know that she looks so obviously, so joyously in love.

When she had finished her fresh fruit in kirsch, Nellie summoned her nerve. It would be easier to call Joy Jones while she was not alone. But she went into the bedroom to use the telephone there.

"Oh, Nellie, at last." Brisk efficient voice which went with the rest of her, handsome, tall, tailored. "Was it you Matthew called last night?"

After about four seconds, Nellie said, "Yes . . ."

"I woke up, it was quite late. I heard him, you know how far away our bedroom is from the living room, but going on and on and I thought I did hear him say your name . . . It was well after two o'clock. I do wish you'd discourage these small-hours ramblings, Nellie. He had to be up at six and he looked terrible, all bloodshot and saggy. I was quite worried about him when he went off."

Was it, merely, a knuckle-rapping? Wifely worry about her husband's losing his sleep? Joy, although amiable enough, looked as if she'd be quite good at rapping knuckles.

Or perhaps a warning, without specifying what Nellie was being warned about. Because the words, the unspeakable facts, could not be brought to the tongue.

Nellie felt her face going red. Trying to control her breathing, she said, "He cost me some sleep too but I thought I was doing a kindness. But yes, next time, if there is one, I'll tell him to go straight to bed."

"There's a dear," said Joy, who was sixteen years her junior. "Sometimes it *must* be a strain being everybody's pal, the way you are. Good night then, Nellie. Take care."

"Anything important?" Charmian asked. "That woman runs her life so well she scares me. Walter's always holding her up as an example. Those dinner parties for twenty, and everything going like clockwork."

"No, nothing important." Nellie hoped the color of fear and of a little anger had left her face. "She's probably just missing Matthew."

Over coffee, which they drank in the long living room with its twinkling, sweeping purple-and-gold view exactly centered by Washington Square Arch, Charmian asked another favor.

Walter, she said, always, when the painters descended, did a general checkup on the contents of the apartment, seeing what if anything needed to be repaired, replaced, or restored. His inventory included an examination of the Lyle storeroom in the basement. Last month her ex-roommate, finally redecorating after five years, had sent her the little desk she had grown up with and took with her everywhere she lived.

"It's not worth a thing but it's pretty and I've always loved it. I have no place for it up here and dear tidy Walter will want to either give it or throw it away—he doesn't believe in unused possessions. Is there any corner at your apartment where it could be tucked in, on loan you might say?"

Nellie considered. "If it's not too big, it might just do for my little front hall, which has always looked a bit naked . . . yes, I can use it."

"I'll get our nice Mr. Jove to bring it over and carry it up. I cleaned it out a bit but the big drawer is filled with things I couldn't decide whether to throw away or not. Next time I'm over I'll finish the job."

"A little clutter will be nothing new in my life." Still with half her mind weighing every word Joy had said, she added absent-mindedly, "If there are any old diaries or love letters tied up in ribbons I promise not to read them."

"How, by the way," Charmian asked, refilling their demitasse cups, "is your sweet Jeremy?"

It probably was the idle, friendly question it sounded like. But coming right on the heels of love letters— It couldn't be possible, could it, that Jeremy was Amanda? But anything was possible. They'd met often. And Charmian was ravishing, there was no denying that.

Oh lord, *no,* Nellie thought. She so badly wanted Jeremy for Ursula. Or rather, she so badly wanted Ursula for Jeremy.

No matter how unpropitious, as of now, the prospect of the coupling looked.

"He's very well. But then he always is." With a sudden sense of urgency she drank down her coffee. Her telephone might be ringing right now. Where are you, Nellie? I've got to talk to you, Nellie.

Charmian was reluctant to let her go. "But I must, some clothes to wash, a button to sew on, and a broken zipper to see to."

"Yes, I remember, from long ago, when I was a working woman," Charmian said a little wistfully. "I could write a whole handbook entitled *Mending with Safety Pins.*"

"And I'll do the sequel, *More Mending with Scotch Tape.* Good night, and thanks."

Nellie walked home very fast. Don't think, don't concentrate, here on the street, don't read messages into footsteps. Wait until there are four walls around you.

After climbing to her apartment, she turned on all the lamps and was for the first time truly grateful for the company of Titania. Such a large animal, and when she barked such a deep organ sound, not reassuring to a stranger outside the door.

Sitting waiting for the telephone to ring, she forced herself into the put-off thinking session.

She was a woman of fortitude and experience and had had her share or more than her share of the dark moments of existence. She had held the hand of the dying, had been called in to

organize things when a very dear friend had committed suicide
and was still lying in the bathtub in a pool of rosy water. She
had had, from the age of twenty-five to forty, the care of an ail-
ing paralyzed father; what might have been her marriage years
went down the drain. Pain and death were not unfamiliar
companions.

What, she thought—if Joy Jones had heard all or part of
Matthew's story last night or, if she hadn't, had heard the loaded
portion of it before—what would I do to Nellie Hand if I were
Joy Jones?

Mentally, she moved into Joy's home, Joy's world. A very well
paid job with a public relations firm. Matthew made plenty, but
their living standards were high. Eight-room Park Avenue apartment. Maid and cook. Designer clothes for Joy, Galanos, Halston,
Blass. She loved her work and was good at it. Very fond of Matthew, in a tolerant and sometimes teasing way, but also needing
and valuing the proper equipment for a woman: an impressive-
looking, highly presentable, successful husband. The serene, firm
ordering of her days, her life, not to be interfered with. "I do
have this awful habit of commanding," Joy said, "but then my
father was a five-star general."

Say—just to be brutally direct about it—that an unimportant
middle-aged saleslady in the Village had it in her power to bring
the whole shining edifice down around her head. Her husband
a convicted murderer. Everything, overnight, gone, smashed.
Good-bye to his seventy-five thousand a year. And, faces in the
papers and on the television screen, even her job, her income,
gone. But these, the financial, were relatively small losses. In
essence, her whole life in smoking ruins.

I would, Nellie-Joy thought, have to get rid of her, neatly,
quickly, once and for all.

How?

Arrange something that looked like an accidental death. Perhaps a shove down the stairs. Or, on a crowded subway plat-
form, the hand in the small of the back as a train came roaring
into the station.

Oh God, Nellie's eyes on the telephone implored, *ring*. You
can put an end, right away, to all this wild morbid nonsense. I

can't blame menopause for my vapors, that's all over and done with.

Poison. In any sort of accidental or deliberate termination of Nellie Hand's life, there would be no connection with Joy to be made. Except by Matthew, and of course he wouldn't count. Just slip into her apartment while she's at work and plant some deadly dose, in the coffee can or the apricot preserves . . . How many keys had she lent, over the years, to people? People wanting to borrow her apartment during the day, as Charmian now wanted to, or while she was away on vacation. Or requiring, for various reasons, a night or two or five on the folding cot she kept for such emergencies.

It wouldn't be hard at all. If it had to be done. If.

There was always the possibility that all Joy had heard was the distant deep buzz-buzz of Matthew, from the living room. That, after registering annoyance and deciding to deliver a scolding to the other party on the line, she had turned over and gone back to sleep. Blissfully, beautifully ignorant.

That left only Matthew to face, in her racing mind. He could use any and all of Joy's methods, and add some of his own. He was big, powerful. His hands already had—

She heard a small involuntary sound escape her. The hands were there before her inner vision, large, square, the big shapely nails buffed and immaculate, the skin pink. A half-inch of striped white cuff showing, the discreet flash of gold cuff links, stylized lions' heads.

Hands that touched her shoulders, lightly, when they met and he bent to kiss her cheek. Hands that had poured her a drink, patted the back of her head— "Don't ever tidy up your hair, Nellie, I love it when it looks as if you've been standing in a wind tunnel."

Hands on the throat of someone named Roy Cox, the thumbs tightening patiently, inexorably, irremovably. Killing him because "you do see there's nothing else I could have done? It was my whole life that was at stake."

By his own free will, however obsessed and driven and needing expiation he was, he had placed it at stake again.

From his, or his wife's, or their mutual point of view, the danger would be there from second to second, terrifyingly real, looming—

All Nellie had to do was open her mouth.

In her turn unburdening herself. "I couldn't stand it, I just had to tell someone."

Their. The two of them, probably one seen, the other unseen. Much easier, surer, more efficient, and after all it was both their lives she had at her disposal.

It was nine o'clock now. Six out there. If he was out there, and not on his way downtown. Surely he'd choose the night hours, when she was alone.

Her apartment seemed to fold itself in its own quiet in spite of the sounds coming up from Timothy Street. At the front, under her windows, was a discotheque named the Evil Hour. A long flight of stairs led down from the sidewalk and when the door was opened, as it increasingly was now, a burst of music as urgent as a scream poured out. At the far end of the block was Trefusa's, a noted and rowdy lesbian restaurant, where tourists paid ten dollars each for tough steak and watery spaghetti to study the interesting specimens at close range. Although Timothy was three blocks west and south of the hub, Eighth Street, it was a busy, noisy street until four. Nellie's ears had long since learned to blank out the sounds but now she found herself listening eagerly for them.

On impulse, she went to the phone and dialed Jeremy's number. She had no idea whatever what she was going to say to him but she needed his vocal presence.

Fortunately or unfortunately, he was not at home. Would she have told him then and there?

Her inability to answer this, her unreal floating feeling, frightened her. She knew she was not a woman guided by logic; but as now by impulse. And by instinct, which dictated her actions and reactions, sometimes guiding her aright and sometimes all wrong.

What if she had poured it out, and Jeremy, concerned for her safety, had demanded that she go immediately to the police? And drive the knife home, deep into Matthew, before she'd had time to consider, to weigh all the consequences. Or before she was even sure whether or not his confession had any foundation in fact.

At ten thirty in desperation she called Ursula Winter. She had to hear a voice. "I've been expecting a call from Matthew and I've been out to dinner—I wondered if he'd called you and left a message."

"No," Ursula said. "No, he didn't."

As a distracted afterthought, thinking about Charmian, Nellie asked, "Jeremy wouldn't by any chance be there?"

"Not by any chance," Ursula said, tone unusually crisp and firm, for her.

At twelve, Nellie checked the locks and reluctantly closed her bedroom windows, although the one next to the fire escape was fitted with a heavy chain link screen.

She probably wouldn't sleep. But if she did, he wouldn't hesitate to wake her at any hour. Just as he always had, before.

Five

Nellie loved her nephew Jeremy better than anyone else in the world. He was possessed of some virtues and she attributed to him the entire list. He was attractive, and she thought him a cynosure. He was talented, and she gave him more: a streak of genius. He was intelligent, and on occasion amusing, and always with her good company; and she declared he was the most delightful creature ever born.

"Delightful" was a word she sometimes thought of in connection with Ursula Winter too. It had seemed the most practical of ideas—when in February Ursula had terminated a long grindingly unhappy love affair that was going nowhere—to bring the two together. She sensed under Ursula's protective garment of blitheness her loneliness and emotional loss. Let's see, had they met before? Just once, she thought, at Matthew and Joy's, at a dinner party, but Ursula was with her man then, and Jeremy with one of his spectacular girls.

He was nominally a fashion photographer but his range was a good deal wider. His work was as individual as his thumbprint and he had begun to make his name and corresponding income in his mid-twenties. He had stayed comfortably on his high perch ever since, as other names, other vogues, came and went. He was thirty-five, just the right age, Nellie judged, for Ursula, whom she guessed was in her late twenties. But in some timeless and intriguing way, older than her age, than her era. In spite of her problems and setbacks, common to every other young woman, mysteriously wiser.

In a manner both direct and devious, she invited the two separately to dinner one Sunday evening in early March. Mustn't be heavy-handed about delicate matters like this. Just a quiet little dinner, her deep-dish steak and kidney pie with the golden bis-

cuit crust, which he always fell upon as though starved. An allow-
ably extravagant bunch of anemones on the little round dining
table at the window. Candlelight, which would make Ursula's
pretty hair look prettier. Have it seem like a sudden impulse,
two nice people joining her on a night that turned out to be conveniently, cozily raining.

In her eagerness and her naivete, she had given herself away
almost from the start of her project.

To Ursula: "How about dropping up for dinner Sunday?
Jeremy may or may not be here—and you and he more or less in
the same business, I thought it would be fun for you, you'd have
so much to talk about."

Ursula was a fashion illustrator, working free-lance for Bonwit
Teller and for several expensive mail-order houses. She did this
work to support a now much more important occupation, to
her: writing and illustrating a children's book, the first one she
had embarked on.

To Jeremy: "My friend from the third floor, Ursula Winter,
may be there. Oh, of course you met her at the Joneses' . . . such
a nice girl. She's come loose from a mooring"—let him know
Ursula was uncommitted—"and needs cheering up. But then it's
the time of year most people do."

Jeremy was fond of his aunt and managed it, even though he
had to cut short a party given by his friend the jazz pianist
Minden Mooney, at which he was having a very good time sharing Minden's piano. He told the girl he left behind him that this
thing was obviously going on for hours, he'd pick her up there
later.

Ursula was there to answer his ring when he arrived half an
hour behind time. She was wearing a black silk shirt and pants.
In the light from a dozen candles placed around the room—oh
bless me, Jeremy thought, taking in the set at a glance—she was a
sort of ghostly white. Her face was narrow and high cheekboned,
with witty eyes, the color impossible to distinguish in the golden
gloom, and an eloquent intelligent mouth. Her hair was a soft
polished light red, parted on one side over the broad white forehead and hanging straight to a little below her faintly crooked
jawline.

"If he's late, and it's a man, it has to be Jeremy," Nellie called from the kitchen, where a delicious scented steam enveloped her head. "Say hello to each other, he knows where the bottles are, good evening, Jeremy."

The candles, the informal little dinner for just the three of them—two of them being people who just barely knew each other, but of opposite sexes—had already sent their message to Ursula. She felt uncomfortable and in the wrong role from the moment he came in. Put up on the block by kind Nellie. Look at this nice young woman. She's available or she wouldn't be here. Isn't she attractive? Isn't her red hair pretty? Wouldn't you like to know her better?

They exchanged smiles and helloes and then he went past her into the kitchen to hug Nellie. He was somewhere between sober and mildly euphoric and found the situation, if a little ridiculous, fascinatingly whispering of forgotten schemes and ceremonies. He prepared himself to be amused.

Nellie emerged from the kitchen as he, sitting on the arm of the sofa, made himself pleasant to Ursula in her slipper chair at right angles to it. She felt his amusement, understood it, and as a result offered her coolest sociable facade to him.

She resented his patient and owlish, determined courtesy. She wasn't used to men making a kind effort to be nice to her.

"Let's see, Nellie said you're a fashion illustrator. Altman's."

"Bonwit Teller."

"But you should sign your work, people do these days."

"I do sign it."

"My God, I did know your last name and now I—"

"Winter."

"You say it in a somewhat onomatopoeic way," he murmured. "But I don't blame you, considering. Mine is Orr."

"Yes, I know." Don't add it. Or yes, do; it looks pointless, sulky, rude, not to: "I like your work. Admire it, rather."

"Thank you. I must make a point of watching out for yours."

How nicely they're coming along, Nellie thought. Chatting away like old friends. She took her head out of the kitchen door and started on the salad and then said, "Oh heavens, no thyme. T-h-y-m-e, we have plenty of time for drinks and dinner."

"Not I, Nellie, I'm due back uptown in an hour," Jeremy said.

"Oh, then, I'll just run down to Basil's now, for my thyme. That does sound funny, doesn't it, Basil and thyme." Flushed and happy at what she thought was such a good beginning, she left them alone. Perhaps ten minutes downstairs with Basil . . .

He doesn't dress like a photographer, Ursula was thinking. Dark easy well-cut suit, perhaps put on as a compliment to his aunt. Compact, working body under it, agile and graceful. A rich warm color that could have been New York's winter status tan but which had probably been acquired on assignment in some hot place; he didn't look like a man who worried about his status. Complicated bony face, merry dark eyes under a gravely formal high forehead. His wide flexible mouth was now in a half-smile as Nellie, in her long mauve chiffon dress with a mauve tippet ruffled in chartreuse, exited.

He emitted a light smiling sigh, meeting her eyes, and she picked up the cue and echoed it. He went to the window and looked out at the rain. "The Dolly Levi of Timothy Street," he said. Ursula's unreliable white skin showed the rising pink under it. But it didn't matter. He wasn't looking at her.

"This reminds me," she said in her soft lifting voice with its fastidious enunciation, "of a sexual experiment Robert Benchley said he once conducted."

"Sexual experiment?" Jeremy turned around. "Nellie?"

"He decided to leave a bicycle and a newt all alone, unchaperoned, one night in his garage and see what would happen. When he went to look next morning, nothing at *all* had happened. The newt had dried up and he accepted scientific defeat and drove away on the bicycle."

He gave her a glance of dark sparkling surprise and enjoyment. "Women's lib or not, I'd assume I'm the bicycle. You must be the newt. I could have wished a better fate for you."

Basil wasn't at home and Nellie thought it would be foolish, in her chiffon, to linger on the drafty stairs. In any case, it would be too soon for them to . . . even though it was said that love could strike like lightning at first sight, and this was more or less first sight . . .

Give a warning anyway. Outside the door, she announced loudly, "I'm back."

"Just in time to help restore Ursula's self-esteem," Jeremy said. "She's for some reason comparing herself to a small salamander."

How nice, little private jokes between them already.

But he had taken his leave right after coffee, saying to Nellie's hope, Nellie's other guest, the polite and nonbinding "See you, Ursula."

Not one to abandon easily any project important to her, Nellie persisted. "Have you heard from that nephew of mine?" No.

She kept him abreast, by telephone, of Ursula's activities. Had he seen her almost double-page spread in the Sunday *Times*? And she, Nellie, had dropped down to borrow some gin for Enid and there was Ursula, working on her children's book, called *The Buttercup Express*. The illustrations were perfectly charming . . . oh, and Ursula had asked for him.

Not she, he thought. Not that girl with her straight proud carriage and high-held head, and her pale, knowing face. She stayed in some distant corner of his brain, though. She had left something with him that was agreeably like a cool, tart taste on the tongue.

If at first you don't succeed— But perhaps make it a little less obvious this time. Jeremy was after all clever, quick, good at reading her mind, and there was a vague possibility he might have suspected his Aunt Nellie was up to something.

Enid provided the opportunity. On a dark windy Thursday, she demanded of Nellie, "Well, tomorrow's the day. Aren't you going to cook up some kind of celebration for me?"

Nellie, who was hanging up a new batch of mattress ticking shopping bags on a gilded coat rack, mentally sought the grounds for the proposed celebration. The anniversary of the founding of the shop? Enid's birthday? The anniversary of one of several long-ago weddings? She didn't like to ask, it would sound tactless.

"Yes indeed. I don't think I can run to dinner, the table is too small, and I know you hate things on laps—"

"To hell with dinner," Enid said gaily. "A nice bottle or two. Let's hope Lise can make it. And be sure to ask my Jeremy."

She described herself as his associate aunt. Several years ago, for pleasure and not a penny, he had shot a black-and-white of her, the long eager eagle face thrust through a tangle of pleated white skirts hanging in the shop window. As Enid was in her

way a local landmark, the photograph was reproduced in the
Village Voice and the *Villager* and she used it on the shiny pink
postcards she mailed for her semiannual clearances.

"Basil, certainly," Enid commanded, with a flourish of her long
ebony cigarette holder. "The dear fascinating crook, I do wonder
where he gets the money to live the way he does. Surely not
from those copies of his."

"Be careful, you just missed burning a hole in the Wilroy,"
Nellie said. "Yes, Basil, and Ursula."

"Odd girl. Let us thank God for it in a relentlessly even world,
all of them now stamped out in Detroit, hair, eyes, jeans, voices.
Nineteen-whatever model, if lost or strayed don't try to find them
because they look like everybody else."

Lukie—or for the moment, Lulu, your niece, doesn't any more
look like anybody else, Nellie thought fleetingly. But then she
apparently has a good reason for it.

Ursula was working on her *Buttercup Express* when she got
her invitation. She studied a finished drawing, spidery pen-and-
ink and dashing flung-on watercolor. The Stationmaster.

How odd. He looked exactly like Jeremy Orr. Eyebrow for
eyebrow, lip for lip, and the same glossy rough chestnut hair
looking as if his fingers had just been run through it.

She thought she had succeeded in dispensing of him mentally.
Three weeks of nothing, since the evening arranged for them by
the Dolly Levi of Timothy Street. You can't, she assured herself,
win them all, Ursula.

Nellie's plot had worked, for her, in some mysterious and unfortunate fashion. Worked in approximately one hour and fifteen
minutes.

The right hands, eyes, brow, voice. The right unseen everything behind the eyes, words and feelings though unspoken felt
through the skin and into the blood. A tough man in his polite
way, but with all his inquiring, testing tendrils in the air: watching, measuring, listening to other people, which was rare in the
self-enclosed world. And the dark glance, laughing, relishing eyes
that she could almost remember from dreams, or childhood.

How out of date, this business of first sight. Of startled recognition. Bringing with it a sharp bright new edge to any day you

woke to. And a feeling of possible unexplored rosinesses around some corner.

Nothing.

"Yes, I'd like to, Nellie," she said, forcing her attention to what was real. "If you're short of cheese, I just bought half a pound of Caerphilly. I'll bring it along, shall I?"

"Enid insisted upon Jeremy," and then in the tone of an anxious mother, "That marvelous-looking new black of yours . . ."

Jeremy, who several nights before had received his sixth bulletin about Ursula, thought it was time to tidy things up. He well knew Nellie's staunch hopeful persistence. "Never say die, Jeremy." That girl, by her very nature, obviously had no part in the maneuvering. He imagined that her quiet white rage, if she found out about Nellie's unblushing salesmanship, would be something to see.

But it wasn't fair to her even if she didn't know.

He arrived at Nellie's with his young actress Anya Mann. "When we get there, you be all over me," he instructed her. "And I, likewise."

"That won't be hard," Anya Mann said. "Even though I did think I'd seen and heard the last of you. It's been weeks."

Ursula was finishing up a last-minute rush job for Bonwit's and was going to have to be late. She was dressed, though, and brushed and scented. Oh hell, why not? she had asked herself. One last time. And thanks for the memory. Whose memory of whom?

It wasn't Susan Tingle of Bonwit's on the telephone, it was Nellie. Voices in the background, laughter. "Aren't you coming up?" The question emerged as a pretext.

"Everybody's here but you. Basil keeps asking for you. And Jeremy has such a . . . such an interesting girl with him. She's the lead in something called *Moon over Nowhere*. She gave me two tickets to it." Her unhappy floundering halted.

"Five minutes, Nellie," Ursula said.

On clear impulse, and without any hesitation, she went into her bedroom and took off the bare black linen dress with the bows on the shoulders, removed her black sandals, went into the bathroom and with soap and washcloth dispensed with any trace of Patou's Joy. She shook her groomed hair carelessly loose, took a paper tissue to the faint delicate green on her eyelids, shed her softly chiming golden bell earrings, and put on white duck pants with a stain of pink and green watercolor on one narrow hip, and a clean but frayed white linen shirt.

She used her glasses only for close fine work; but she decided to wear them. They were large and round, with tortoise rims, and gave her expressive face a misleading studious, solemn look.

Nobody, she informed her optically blurred reflection in the door mirror, has to tell you anything twice. Or considering the lapse of weeks since the candlelit zero dinner, a dozen times. But for God's sake take that forsaken look away from your mouth.

Later, she remembered very little, except for the occasional flash, about the party for Enid.

It turned out that what they were celebrating was Enid's release from jail, where she had spent twenty-four hours after dumping a can of house paint over the head of a shouting young man in a Nazi uniform who happened to pause conveniently under her apartment window.

Oh yes. That must be Jeremy's girl. Anya something. Floaty white crepe de Chine slit to the waist in front, but breasts so far apart they only, creamily, hinted at themselves. Nosegay of white violets where the dress finally came together. "Ah," Basil said, saluting her with his glass, "a lady in white. Delicious. Virginal!"

Lise Kozer, leaning heavily on a stick, monopolizing her hostess. "Yes, a drink, but first if it wouldn't be too much trouble, Nellie, a cup of tea. I trust you have Earl Grey, and I like it steeped four minutes. And as I haven't eaten all day perhaps some thin toast with just a breath of butter. I've brought along a pot of caviar, you might spread some on the toast."

Walter Lyle, never at home at parties, particularly Village parties, eyes on Charmian wherever in the room she happened to be. Ursula overheard Anya murmuring to Jeremy, "Rather attractive, that blond woman." On the sofa beside her, he bent in laughter and said, "Yes, as they say of the Mona Lisa, not bad . . ." Anya gave him a wide-eyed puzzled stare.

Walter fell to, or rather offered himself as, Ursula's lot. It was unnerving talking to him when he wasn't, except for a quick flicker, looking at you. At Nellie's dinner, Jeremy had said, "If you took a color shot of Walter Lyle he'd come out a black and white." He was of medium height, and gave an impression of being strung on wires, not flexible but tensely rigid wires. Somewhere in his forties, she supposed. Pale taut skin, retreating flat smooth dark hair, lightless eyes as close to black as she had ever seen, mathematically perfect features. Handsome in his way, coldly sure of himself if not of what his wife might be up to, six feet away. He had now, as always, a habit of glancing at his watch repeatedly, as though precious executive time was being wasted.

Enid, nearby, hearing him talking about Atlantic seaboard off-shore oil rights, and the mulish blindness of the citizenry opposing them, took pity and came over. And then Basil did, and then Nellie, and then Jeremy. Ursula, drinking fast and thirstily, found herself to her extreme annoyance being amusing, eliciting laughter from all around her. Her cheeks felt too hot. She had the sense of unreality that accompanies a fever.

"But is this my pensive Ursula?" Basil cried, as usual with the volume to fill Nellie's and possibly the next-door apartment. "You flame, you glow! Let us not waste your sweetness upon the desert air—forgive me, Nellie—let us go down to my rooms of state and drink vodka with essence of cucumber. And I will show you"—he gave a deep dramatic sigh—"my imitations."

Damn it, Ursula thought, I will not flame and glow. She went into the kitchen to slice more Caerphilly cheese. Right outside the door, Anya said, "You really are a sexy man, did you know that?"

"Last thing that would ever occur to me," Basil roared. "But tell me more about the man I love. If you're not careful I'll take *you* down to see my imitations. Or if that man of yours isn't careful."

Uncertainly, "Are you a mime?"

"No, a painter. A human Xerox. Would you by any chance be interested in a perfectly executed Hogarth's *The Shrimp Girl?* I'd let you have it for five hundred dollars, not including the frame. Stage people, take it from me, are imbeciles about art. They'd never know the real thing was hanging large as life in the National Gallery in London."

"I would love to see your . . . paintings, if we didn't have to run."

Jeremy, following an impulse he knew to be cross-grained and contrary, and possibly the result of three leisurely but powerful martinis, came into the kitchen and said, "Ursula, you're wrong."

"Wrong about what?" She arranged English water crackers on a plate, eyes intent on them.

"I tried that Benchley experiment in my own garage. The bicycle and the newt mated and produced a very small tricycle, with a tail, to pull along a little red wagon with."

He saw for the first time her face opening to him, to the tune of her spontaneous soft rush of laughter. Her widening fine eyes he now discovered to be somewhere between green and sapphire, a lighted underwater color.

A claiming white hand slipped over his shoulder from behind. "Come on, darling, we're late."

"Good-bye, Jeremy," Ursula said, unscrewing the cap from a jar of gherkins. "As they say, see you."

Six

As always when she woke deep in the night—and this was the fourth waking, this silent night—Nellie made mental lists of things she would do the next morning, the next day. It was always soothing and now it was more than soothing: it helped to put a hedge around the unknown.

Four-thirty. It's one-thirty in California. Hurry, get to the list.

Up at seven. The coming morning would be an egg morning; she allowed herself two eggs a week. Scrambled, with a touch of parsley flakes? Or boiled, with a squeeze of fresh lemon to remove the New York egginess, not quite a country taste.

Coffee. There was just enough for one cup, she must remember to pick up a two-pound can, and chicory to stretch it with, at that scandalous price. But she liked the faint aromatic bitterness of the chicory anyway.

(In her ear, Jeremy's voice said, "For God's sake, Nellie, a hundred extra, or fifty, or even forty a week? It's no problem, I'd like to." "Thank you, Jeremy, but I'm far happier on my own, it's a kind of game with me to manage on what I make. When and if I get a bit pressed . . . but thank you anyway, dear.") Independence had been bred in her bones.

Walk Titania. Pick up another bag of her dry dog food.

She remembered that one shoulder strap was broken on the blue slip she proposed to put on. It had popped while she was waiting on a customer last week. There is nothing, Nellie thought, more harum-scarum-looking than a semidetached slip strap hanging out of a dress sleeve. A small safety pin would have to do.

How pleasant it would be, after this long darkness, this sense of being alone in a whispering cave where unseen things scuttled and odd small noises terrified—how pleasant to be among crowds of everyday people on the street, people without a care in the world.

Or at least just ordinary cares: the rent, or having to have one shoe heeled, or being late for work, or wondering if they were going to keep their job, or what their wife or husband was up to, or whether the pain in the chest was indigestion or something unnameable. But at least, not worrying minute to minute about whether it might be in someone's interest to do away with them.

Safe people, near enough to touch, near enough to be asked for help. In a half-sleep, she reached out a hand. There was Joy Jones walking along the sidewalk with her, except that to everyone else she was absolutely unrecognizable. Jeans on her long legs, a tousled blond wig, she could be anyone, she could be everyone . . .

Her head jerked on the pillow. Lukie in disguise yesterday. "He doesn't know where I work. I think we're safe. For the time being." Safe from what?

Let's see, where was she, in her list? Her shower. There was only a sliver in the soap dish; remember to unwrap a fresh cake so she wouldn't have to get out dripping to do it.

The tapestry-printed cotton suit, she'd wear that; not too warm, not too cool. "All right, I admit it's another mistake," Enid said. "You can have it for five dollars. Forget the sales tax." It was good sturdy cloth, it had already lasted three years, and the colors were cheerful.

Pick up Lise's capsules at Bigelow's, and drop them off. Lise could have had them delivered but she didn't like to answer the doorbell in her old pink robe, clean but graying with age. "But let us be patient, Nellie. Soon I shall have white velvet and marabou to answer the door in. And so shall you."

Noises, faint, from the back courtyard four stories down sent her to the window. A car, someone getting out, being careful not to slam the door. Someone whose feet might now begin steadily, silently, to climb the fire escape. Wire cutters feeling their way through the heavy protective screen at her window. But there would be plenty of time to scream, and windows were open, it was a balmy night—

It wasn't a car, it was—as far as she could distinguish in the dim light—a van, backed up to the rear door of Basil's apartment.

She thought she saw him in the doorway. Packages, pale, large, flat, being handed in by another vague figure. She couldn't imagine what they could be but frames. Odd hour to accept delivery of merchandise, but then Basil was odd, a law unto himself; he never did things other people's ways and at other people's times.

Jeremy occasionally amused himself by speculating to her on the mysterious, affluent Basil. "D'you suppose his gallery could be a dope drop? On the way here"—this had been in bitter January—"I saw him in a double-breasted black coat with a mink collar and lapels and I'll swear it was lined in mink. Against the cold." Or, "Maybe he distills two hundred proof vodka in his basement. All you need is potato peelings, or rinds, any old thing. Could he be making five-hundred-dollar bills? He keeps talking about how well he copies expensive art."

There was no doubt that Basil's apartment was sumptuous, not what you'd expect to find behind the modest doors of Timothy Street. A floor through, the ceilings much higher than in the apartments above. Antique, not antiqued, mirror walls in the living room behind the gallery. A peacock splendor of fur and velvet surfaces, great green fountains of palm in Chinese porcelain tubs, looming lacquered cabinets filled with treasure. A little dining room all in blue and white Persian tile, floors, walls, ceilings, with a lion's head marble fountain on one wall dripping a stream of crystal into the ivy-grown shell basin underneath. "God bless my Aunt Vasia," Basil would cry when his guests gazed in envious admiration. "She may have been mad but her taste was impeccable. For the effete, the decadent, I mean."

Watching at the window, and beginning to shiver a little, Nellie thought that she didn't want to know what, if anything, Basil was up to; and that as it was she knew far too many things about too many people.

With curiously uncertain hands, she got down the Royal Worcester egg coddler Lise had given her. The painted rosy peach and the blackberries gave her a small flick of comfort and pleasure, particularly noticeable because she usually enjoyed every moment of her solitary early mornings. She buttered the coddler, broke an egg into it, added lemon juice, a pinch of bay, salt and pepper, and placed it in boiling water.

No matter what they said about men, about marriage, it was not without compensation to sit with your hair like a mare's nest, no one across the table to see you, the *Times* to read without having to chat.

Although for the first five pages there was little serenity to be garnered. More ghastliness in Rhodesia, and only the beginning, she thought. Twenty-nine die in Bronx hotel fire. Daughter and wife of U. S. Ambassador to Egypt taken as hostages, will die in twenty-four hours unless—

Robberies, not the little ones that happened as regularly as the streets' heartbeats, but spectacular coups. A quarter of a million dollars' worth of jewels, from a new East Side condominium where the tightest security was claimed to be maintained. Paintings from the storerooms of the Frick, the impregnable Frick. A barnful of antique cars stolen from the country estate of a famous pop singer in Greenwich, Connecticut. How could people just drive away in antique cars and not be stopped? How could people do any of the outrageous impossible things they were doing in the *Times* and get away with it? But they did.

Hostages. The stony cruelty of it, someone you loved perhaps to suffer torture, to die. Unless you arranged the release of some sort of prisoners or could put your hand on five million, ten million dollars or could summon up a 747 for transport to somewhere. Someone you love—

There was a clutching feeling around her heart. What a good way to keep Nellie quiet. Use Jeremy. Everybody knows she's crazy about her nephew Jeremy. Haven't you heard her talking about him?

Go on like this and you won't be able to move, to eat, to think, to function at all. With a long shaky sigh, she turned to the unharrying daily joys of the *Times:* book review, editorials, theater and dance. But the play reviewed was about a man and his stepson both intent on murdering the man's wife, neither knowing the other's plan.

When, the animals' needs attended to, she went down the stairs for the second time, she was startled to see a young man waiting in a corner of the small dark hall, just inside the door.

He was very tall and very thin and looked as though he had been dipped, all of him, in a strong bleach. Colorless hair, eyes, eyebrows, in this light, long blade of face with gaunt cheeks and a powerful lopsided jawline, white pants, a little soiled, white turtleneck jersey.

"You're her," he said, moving from the corner where he had been leaning. "Nellie something."

Nellie moved past him and got the door halfway open. She said breathlessly, "Yes, what do you want?" Without her thinking about it her fingers went to her coral necklace, which had been her mother's, surely not worth more than forty or fifty dollars but still—

"Is she up there or has she left for work? I know she works somewhere."

"Is who up there?"

"Lukie." Carefully, he amplified, "Lucinda Callender."

"No, she isn't, and hasn't been."

"I heard she said she was. I heard she said she'd be staying with you." He moved again. He was only a foot away from her. "Suppose you just lend me your keys, I'll run up and see, you can have them back in a minute or two."

She heard the splash of water on the sidewalk. She shot out the door, tripped over Basil's hose, and almost fell. He caught her just in time and she gasped, "Basil, a man, a boy, in the hall," and could and needed to get no farther. Armed with his hose and its no-nonsense stream of water, Basil jerked the door wide. The hall was empty. To the right of it a narrow dim corridor led to the back of the building and to a door which once in grander days had been the trade and delivery entrance. This door could be opened from the inside. It was open now.

"So. Doughty Nellie scares a villain away," Basil said. "Get on to work, I'll keep an eye out. Just tell me what he looks like."

Nellie did, accurately, finding it a help because she was trying to keep back tears. Why, suddenly, was everything so terrifying? Where had her stability, her common sense, gone to? Even Basil looked frightening, with forearms tensed, fists balled at his sides.

But I can't, she thought, I can't go to work, not right now. He may follow me, he may think or guess she works where I work if she said she was staying with me. Go to Lise's with the bottle of capsules and linger over another cup of coffee? No, he could follow me there, and rob her.

Enraged at her fears, her helplessness—"God helps those who help themselves," intoned her Aunt Bess; she had always thought it a singularly uncharitable saying—she walked rapidly down Timothy and made a swift passage, not daring to look over her shoulder, to the yawning mouth of the Eighth Street station of the IND subway on Sixth Avenue. A northbound E train was just thundering in, but it didn't matter which train it was. The worst of the morning crush, now at nine forty-five, was over, but there were masses of seethingly noisy adolescents, staggered school hours, she supposed; she almost never took the subway at this hour. Because she was always safely and happily walking to work at this hour.

He wasn't, at least, in this car of the E train. She mentally cursed Lukie in as strong language as she could summon. Oh dear, oh honestly, that was very wrong of you, Lukie. You may be able to handle your friends, but I can't.

There was a rending screech as the E train swung east at Radio City. Nellie got out at Fifty-third and Fifth Avenue, glad of the jam of scholars on the escalator with her. She walked very fast, and would have run except she thought it would look odd, to Fifty-first and went in at the side entrance to St. Patrick's Cathedral. As she passed the center of the main altar she didn't genuflect, but made a ducking gesture of her head toward the sanctuary. As an Anglican Catholic, she did not subscribe to the doctrine of the Real Presence, but it wouldn't do to offend these silent kneeling people.

Out the opposite side entrance, take a chance jaywalking, dart through the Fiftieth Street door of Saks Fifth Avenue. She lingered at the scarf counter, eyes searching the scantily peopled sales floor; the store had only just opened. There was no bleached boy to be seen.

A fleeting feeling of well-being struck her, of independence and euphoria. She had shaken him, she must have shaken him; poor helpless dithering Nellie had done a good job of getting rid of a possible tail.

Head up, no longer in her bent-over scurry, she walked to the telephone booths at the doors opening onto Forty-ninth Street and called Babylon.

Enid answered. "Nellie, for God's sake, I've been calling and calling you at home—"

Don't explain now. Too complicated. "I'll be there in twenty minutes or so."

"No, under no circumstances. The reason I was calling you was about your horoscope for today." Enid was a close follower of newspaper horoscopes for herself and her friends, and when it was convenient obeyed her own and exhorted others to do the same. "It said 'Danger to dear ones, be faithful and vigilant, and do not put workday cares before real responsibilities.' You'd better go see Lise at once, she may need you and not want to call you."

This seemed unlikely. Lise was not a hesitant summoner of assistance.

Dear ones . . . Oh God, not Jeremy. She reminded herself that she didn't believe in astrology, or at least beyond the muzzy, all-inclusive "There are more things in heaven and earth, Horatio . . ." But it wouldn't hurt to—

"All right, you'll see me when you see me," she said. She hesitated. "I forget—is this one of Lukie's days?" The girl, self-sufficient as she seemed to be, ought to be warned, and as soon as possible. No, Enid informed her, it wasn't, and added, "Pot calling the kettle black, but I could swear from the sound of you, you don't know what day it is, Nellie."

She allowed herself a taxi. Get there quickly, say hello, I just happened to be in your part of town. See that everything was all right, which of course it would be, and then go on downtown by bus.

Jeremy's quarters, working and living, were on East Thirty-first Street. Behind the modest white stucco two-story house, and invisible from the street when the double-doored gate to the right was closed, was a center garden-courtyard with two great ailanthus trees and a fountain in it. And beyond that stood a commodious building, echoing, high-ceilinged, which had once been the Museum of Armenian Art. It was now Jeremy's studio, remodeled to hold darkroom and dressing rooms, and an office for his girl Friday, Peggy Earl.

As Nellie's cab stopped in front of the white house's dark green door, the gate was opened and a mounted policeman clattered into the street.

Nellie heard her own strangled cry and reached for the door handle. "And did it occur to you to pay me, ma'am?" the taxi driver asked in an Irish accent. "I'd like to ferry people around just for the fun of it but—"

Seventy-five cents on the meter. She thrust a dollar on him and got out on shaky legs. "Officer!" she cried. But the horse wheeled smartly around and trotted back in at the gate, hoofs striking urgent fearful noises from the cobblestoned drive within. Following in terror, Nellie saw, in the courtyard, at least ten policemen, and three riderless horses tethered to an ailanthus tree.

She reached for a windowsill in the side wall of the house to support herself and screamed, "*Jeremy!*"

In a half-fainting fading of light she saw a girl in a dress made of floating flame-red chiffon handkerchiefs running toward her. The girl just caught her as her knees deserted her.

In the clearing haze, there was the chiffon girl, and a concerned looking policeman, tall Peggy Earl with a paper cup of water, and a handsome woman in glasses whom she identified later as the designer Pauline Trigere.

Peggy, given to talking in shorthand because she was always so busy, said, "Well, of course. Anyone would. If they didn't know. Come along, Miss Hand, you'll want to sit down. Jeremy's shooting, we'll go to my nook."

Nellie wasn't sure how her legs got her there but in a few moments she found herself sitting in Peggy's colorfully untidy office. The phone was ringing as they went in and Peggy snatched it up and said, "Yes, six pairs of lovebirds, and they must be in the French wicker cages, and four parrots, we don't want any that bite. Ten A.M. tomorrow at the *latest*."

To Nellie, as she poured brandy into small balloon glasses miraculously produced from a desk drawer, she explained, "About the police. J. O. hasn't robbed a bank or hanged himself. A feature for *You* magazine. New York's Finest. Designers, you know. And models in their things. With policemen, and horses. Terrific page layouts, I have them somewhere. Drink up, you're green as a grape."

"Peggy!" Jeremy's voice shouted.

"Coming." She downed her brandy. "Sit still. Take fifteen deep breaths. Reading matter—" The May issue of *Vogue* was dropped in Nellie's lap.

She must have informed Jeremy about his aunt and her condition, because he came running, as close to cross as Nellie had ever seen him. "Nellie, what the *hell*—"

"Sorry, I was worried about you, and then I saw the police, and I . . ."

"Worried about me!" The tense lash in his voice made her blush miserably.

Cancel that, cover it up, it sounded so foolish. "I was on my way down from Saks Fifth Avenue and I just stopped in to see you."

As far as he could recollect she never shopped in expensive midtown stores and never, never dropped in on him.

But there wasn't time to be puzzled, to sort it out. To worry about his inconvenient and intrusive, fainting, blushing aunt. Behaving herself in this uncharacteristic fashion.

"Sorry to snap, I've been at this since five this morning. You'd better get on downtown to your own habitat." Trying, impatiently, to sound kind. He had at least four more hours of shooting before him.

"Peggy, put out the case of beer, I hope it's cold—"

"Are you kidding? Of course. Pilsener glasses chilled, even."

"Halston would like some fresh lemonade, if you can arrange it. With mint." Giving Nellie an absentminded pat on the head, he left them.

"Usually good-natured, though," Peggy said. "For someone so very. Cab for you. *And* an arm."

There were very few taxis on East Thirty-first Street but nothing was impossible to Peggy. She put two fingers between her teeth and emitted a piercing whistle. Not only a taxi, but a big one, a Checker, shot obediently around the corner of Lexington and pulled up.

Getting into it, Nellie said in her young voice, embarrassed and hesitant now—what an ass she had made of herself—"Thank you very much. I will think twice about ever bursting in upon Jeremy again."

Seven

Matthew Jones had had very little time to think about anything after his plane landed at Los Angeles International Airport.

He walked right into the two-day party for the launching of "Momma's House," a new television series made by the Vade Studios, which were one of the numerous holdings of the mighty deVries Bank of New York.

He had as his companions on the plane and intermittently but demandingly from then on, a group of advertising sponsors for the series, to whom he knew he was expected to act as a big-time nursemaid, even though several of his own sales staff had come along to frolic.

The president of Blackstone Industries and his advertising manager, two top executives of Gary Pharmaceutical, and no less than the chairman of the board of the National Electric Company, an agile gentleman of seventy-four. There was a notable shortage of wives; Matthew assumed that they had been told that the Coast journey would mainly consist of meetings and conferences.

Wherever the party went, "Momma's House" went too, the pilot repeating itself interminably on TV monitors at poolside, in living rooms and drinking rooms and bedrooms, on terraces, in rose gardens.

"Momma's House" was about a middle-aged ex-whore with a heart of gold who went around collecting prostitutes, took them off the streets, reformed them, taught them sewing and cooking, and in due time arranged safe happy marriages for them. Of course, Momma had rebels and dropouts, and she had to go after them into steamily sinister places and try to bring them home again, risking her plump neck in the process. Her project had incurred the undying rage of a Mafia chieftain who swore he would arrange her demise. In the pilot, three sailors invaded Momma's house in search of a particularly succulent redhead they remembered as a fixture in Dolan's Bar. And all hell broke loose.

UBC was the highest bidder for the series, even though the material was conceded to be what Matthew called a little dicey. But sex was *it*, these days, on television, now that violence per se had gotten somewhat of a black eye. However, there was room for violence in "Momma's House," violence aimed toward a virtuous purpose, the redemption of the beautiful and damned. And, in close-ups of the horrors Momma's girls were to be rescued from, there was ample opportunity for some nice, raw, make-'em-blush realism.

Matthew never did find out who all his sixty-or-so fellow party-goers were, nor did he care. This was just one of the things you took in stride when you were executive vice president, Sales, United Broadcasting Company. There was the entire cast, of course, and a sprinkling of bankers, battalions of the press, Vade executives, and lovely if unreal-looking girls beyond counting, their function at the celebration never clearly stated but perfectly understood by all.

Matthew was, as always, sourly amused by the spectacle of rich men who could presumably buy anything they wanted, lapping up free drinks and gratis girls.

Joy had been invited too but shuddered. "I can just see it. Orgies are such a bore. For heaven's sake be kind to your stomach, Matthew. No one ever really recovers from an ulcer, you know."

He had long since learned his own survival methods in the entertainment industry. He was a champion drink-stretcher. And well before it became an absolute necessity he switched to lime juice and soda for hours, or iced tea, for which he had a thirsty passion.

The races at Santa Anita. Screenings of highbrow pornographic films at a private studio in Momma's producer's house. Parties starting in the morning, shifting, changing ground. Squads of Cadillacs waiting to transport you from orangery to discotheque, from tennis court to yacht.

He thought it was odd how lonely you could be in the midst

of all the canned merriment. And maybe odder still that it wasn't Joy he found himself from time to time thinking about, and missing, but Nellie. It would be nice to go off into a quiet corner and have a sane conversation with Nellie, a woman at a moon's remove from this vast bash.

It had taken him a year or so after he met her to figure out why she was so important to him. Then out of buried memory had floated up a forgotten vivid picture of his adored sister Meg who had died at ten when he was seven. Meg had borne a strong resemblance to his mother, whom he loved very much. Nellie looked like both of them, sounded like them, was, he was convinced, like them right down to the bone. A home for him to go and live in, every once in a while; mustn't make a nuisance of yourself and overdo it. A safe and sunlit place as it had existed before his father's suicide, before Meg's death, before his mother's life had fallen apart.

Dear Nellie. Standing with his iced tea, talking to Rose Alanna, the actress who played Momma, he thought, I'd trust my life to her.

And then remembered, with a shock that hit his fingertips, I did.

Not that he had forgotten about it, but just hadn't applied these exact words to it.

He had been reasonably sober at the time, but very tired, and once he started telling her he couldn't possibly stop; or having reached a point of no return, as he had known he had, couldn't say, Forgive my ramblings, I'll finish this story another time.

As he talked, relief had flooded his veins and he felt the terrible burden lightening, lifting.

In the cold light of morning, things naturally looked a little different. All right, he had been a damned fool, but by God it had been worth it. For the first time on the anniversary of the . . . the accident of temper, of rage, he had gone off to sleep without dreaming about it.

"Ghastly, don't you think?" asked Momma. He had no idea what she was talking about but said that ghastly was hardly the word for it. He hoped belatedly that she wasn't talking about the show.

When there was something that troubled him deeply, and

required thought or demanded solution sooner or later, he had a habit of storing it away out of mental sight until he could attend to it. Put it on your shelf, Matthew, he would advise himself.

Go back to the door he'd just come in by: I'd trust my life to her.

On the weary evening of the second day of the party, he was deputing Carnelli, of the UBC Sales Department, to see that the chairman of the board was gotten off the top of the discotheque table where he was doing the Charleston all by himself, and seen safely to bed, the sooner the better.

A girl with waist-length black hair interrupted their conference. "You're wanted on the telephone, Mr. Jones. Someone named Benning."

"Someone named Benning!" Carnelli threw back his head and laughed. Rendered chummy by drink, he said to Matthew, "God himself. I hope there's no trouble on high."

Matthew took the call in a phone booth that reeked of cigar smoke and L'Air du Temps. Brandon Benning, President of UBC, said, "Pretty well through with the belly-dancers, Matthew?"

"Just about, thank God, why?"

"Something's come up. I won't go into it now, got a jam of people on my neck— But we've got to get together. Right away. Can you be with me no later than ten tomorrow?" Boardrooms and billions spoke in the soft commanding Virginia voice.

Emergencies were daily bread in this business. But a giant cold hand squeezed Matthew's heart.

Now, what was *this* feeling all about?

"All right, if— You may or may not have been informed that I was going on up to Portland to see about picking up or not picking up that affiliate. I'd scheduled three or four more days out here—"

"Forget Portland for the moment. They'll wait. This is first priority. See you, pal."

One of the obliging Cadillacs drove him back to the Beverly Wilshire Hotel, where while he was hastily packing he stopped to wonder when last he had eaten. Funny hollow feeling inside him, gnawing.

Something's come up.

A smoked salmon and cucumber sandwich at around two, a handful of olives at five. He'd been on iced tea since noon. He ordered from room service martini makings, and got on the telephone to the airlines.

Just as he'd feared, nothing available in first class, not from this stamping ground of the show-off. One coach seat available on American. Okay, cattle car it is, Matthew said grimly to himself, and made a quantity of powerful martinis in the slim silver pitcher provided.

Food too, though; must play this with a clear head. He ordered a steak, rare, asparagus, a broiled tomato, and crème brûlée as a soothing finish for his jumpy stomach.

But what the *hell* was this panic scene all about? He always, deliberately, played the big game with outward calm, never came panting and running when higher-up fingers were snapped at him.

What of great importance to UBC had been pending when he left New York? He searched his mind. Could be that the Legal Department was having second thoughts about "Momma's House"? A viewers' revolt against television sex was just beginning to make a faint timid patter on the roof. A new wizard in law had come in, Wall Street, tough, to, as Brandon Benning put it, straighten up by Christ the spine of the department. And the first airing of "Momma's House" was this coming Saturday at 9 P.M. Yes, that would constitute a ten-alarm emergency.

Yes, that might be it.

He started to eat, couldn't, and then forced himself along bite by bite.

After finishing his third stalk of asparagus, he got up and went to look in the mirror over the white-lacquered French desk to take some kind of bearings.

Shoulders not quite as well held, eyes a bit baggy underneath from late nights, too many liquids if even innocent ones, and held-in boredom. But otherwise okay: tall, well-fleshed, rosy. Self-contained, immaculately turned out, looking, as he arranged his features, patient, aware, and mildly amused.

He went back to begin on his broiled tomato. Another reassuring thought: Dell Dairies might be making trouble. They had threatened to drop "Kissing Cousins" at the end of the first thirteen weeks. Dell's advertising manager was a close friend of Matthew's. Maybe it was felt that his presence might save the day, and at least screw Dell down for a second thirteen weeks, during which time another sponsor could be sought. The ratings were good on "Kissing Cousins," but one woman among millions, the advertising manager's mother, turned it on accidentally one evening, thought it was disgusting, and telephoned her son from Palm Springs. On this slender thread dangled the financial future of many.

Yes, well, maybe. The problem sounded not unlikely and even welcome, trouble with the Cousins.

In the middle of his coffee, he called Joy. "Home tomorrow morning, dear." He had to force himself to add, "How's everything at your end?" and found himself waiting for a wall to crumble and fall on his head.

"Oh, fine. I'm having some people for drinks, mustn't linger too long. Are you all right?"

"Yes, fine. No news? No alarums or excursions to report?"

"You're the only man I know who still pronounces the *u* in alarums. And for that matter the second *i* in liaison. No, if anything wonderful or ghastly has happened concerning us or anyone we know, nobody has told me about it. Yet. Happy trip, Matthew. Do try to get some sleep."

Jammed into that ultimate place of discomfort, the center seat in a row of three, and at the rear of the plane for good measure, Matthew tried desperately to give all his attention to his paperback, *Madame Bovary*, which for some reason he had never read.

It didn't do to start thinking, exhausted as he was, hypnotized as he was by the wasps and bees, the jet engines, which after a time began saying things, words, "Nellie . . . Nellie . . ."

He tried many times and without any kind of success to adjust his long legs to the insufficient space. There was an enormously fat man to his left, by the window, asleep and snoring. When the snores reached an impossible peak, the man gasped, made strangling noises, woke, groaned with a sound of anguish, and then started the cycle all over again. The woman to his right wore a large-brimmed black straw hat and when occasion-

ally her head nodded the brim scraped his cheek. Behind him,
the four w.c.'s were in steady demand.

Nellie. The steady clear blue eyes, the eyes of a girl in her
twenties. Suddenly looking anxious, or even with tears in them.
"It's too much for me, I just had to tell someone, I couldn't bear
carrying it around all by myself. But this is *absolutely* in con-
fidence . . ."

Or, "I need advice, and strange as it may seem it's literally a
matter of life and death. What would you do if you were me?"

She was, he knew, that current rarity, a woman of conscience.
Conscience in this case could work two ways, honorable silence
or the alternative.

She had friends by the dozen, intimates. People whom she was
sure she could trust. Just as he had been sure he could trust her.

Had been sure? *Am* sure. Present tense.

For the fourth time, he read the first line of *Madame Bovary*.
"We were in the study-hall when the headmaster entered, followed by a new boy not yet in school uniform and by the handy-
man carrying a large desk."

This is first priority. See you, pal.

Matthew's pink skin turned rose and then a suffused red.
Christ, summoned to the headmaster's, the principal's office. He
was ten again, and being asked whether he had or hadn't poured
a jar of red poster paint down the back of Hector Agnew's neck
and if he had what was he prepared to say for himself. Heavy
threatening yardstick being tapped on the green desk blotter as
the question was asked.

Did you or did you not commit murder five years ago, pal?
What are you prepared to say for yourself, Matthew?

But they'd never come anywhere near a suspect, the police
hadn't. After all this time, there wasn't the remotest way to con-
nect him with it. There hadn't been anyway directly after it
happened. He had wiped every surface he had touched after
entering the cottage—*hadn't he?*—and anyway his fingerprints
weren't on file; he had never been arrested for anything.

Brandon Benning for reasons of his own personal safety might
have a plainclothes policeman sitting in one corner of his immense office. After he'd put the question—I don't suppose I'd

have a heart attack then and there, Matthew thought, sweat running down his face—the policeman would take over.

One of those people you never see, but who invariably see you, some snooping old crone in a cottage down the road from Roy Cox's, saying, "Yes, that's the man, I remember him. He got out of his car about nine o'clock in front of Mr. Cox's house. He left about half an hour later."

But even if there was no old crone, there was Nellie. Wait now—Nellie would have to have been the *source* of the information, the reason why Principal Benning had him on the mat.

He got up from his seat, the swift motion waking the strawhatted woman. She sighed with fury and moved her legs aside to let him into the aisle. The second w.c. on the left was unoccupied. He went in and threw up all his carefully consumed nourishment. He washed his face and hands and picked up the bottle of Arden for Men and rubbed it on his cheeks and forehead.

In the galley, he stopped and murmured an order for a double scotch. Swallowing it where he stood, he looked down at Chicago, O'Hare Airport directly beneath. Two hours to New York.

The scotch helped, pouring at least a physical sense of ease through his veins and muscles.

You blithering ass, Matthew said to himself. Growing ten years older on a flight from coast to coast. Go back and read yourself to sleep.

Yes, he'd conjured up quite a tempest in the teapot of an ordinary business emergency. Just an ordinary, everyday UBC fire to deal with. To douse. Quench. He was sure he'd be up to it.

Eight

"Sit down, Matthew," Brandon Benning said. "Only one man is allowed to prowl this office like a tiger."

Matthew, with bloodshot aching eyes, examined his face to see what it thought about what was going to be said, but then you never could tell with Benning. He was very tall, and squashed and tennised into a racy limberness of body. Matthew held a theory that he had his wiry curly hair dyed that stone-gray, it went so perfectly with the color of his eyes, and set off so splendidly his year-round tan.

In illustration of his point, Benning walked the width of his office and back, hands in his pockets. It was clear that whatever he was going to say, he was enjoying himself. A dealer with large questions, dispenser of large decisions, taking his time about it. The whole west wall of his office was glass, and the parade of sunlit morning towers was a good backdrop for him.

There was no one, plainclothes-looking or otherwise, in the corner of the office, which measured forty by forty feet.

Matthew sat staring at Benning's desk, which wasn't a desk at all but a round, highly polished ebony wood table, its surface, in a vogue followed by certain executives, absolutely bare, except for the telephone, recessed out of sight, and a half-circle of buttons which when fingered summoned anything that Benning wanted, from television monitor control to the services of the UBC staff doctor.

Benning sat down in his Eames chair, which had been upholstered to order in a Persian silk rug patterned with sea horses and anemones.

"You poor soul," he said. "You look wenched to death, Matthew. I hope you enjoyed it, every minute of it."

Only grimly applied will power kept Matthew quiet in his chair. His head felt as though it were going to burst.

"Do you like it here?" Benning asked. "I don't mean here at UBC, but here in this office? Does it feel right to you?"

What kind of hideous game was he playing, Matthew wondered feverishly. Did anyone like it, in the principal's office? Benning hadn't a ruler, nor a blotter to tap it with, but the feeling was exactly the same.

"Nice office," he managed. "I like a western exposure. The morning sun is a little—"

"You could always have it curtained, in any case." Benning never fell into the trap of drapes or draperies. "Though the view at night—I'm afraid there's a lot of night work involved—is worth the price of admission."

Matthew, who had given up smoking a year ago, patted his right-hand pocket in vain.

Uncannily, Benning read the gesture. He pulled open a curved drawer and tossed a pack of Marlboros across the table. "One won't hurt you. Under the circumstances."

He didn't dare go through the motions of opening the pack, getting out a cigarette, and lighting it. His hands would be seen shaking. God, was his *head* beginning to tremble on his neck?

"The thing is," Benning said softly, "that if a few more cards are played right, and I'm sure they will be, this is going to be your office, Matthew."

He showed his teeth in a dour white grin. "I'm moving up. My ass still hurts from the feel of those boots, promoting me. I am to be managing consultant to UBC, whatever that means. I wanted a friend in this chair, not some nosegrinder who thinks he can well do without a managing consultant."

Matthew heard the rest of it only dimly, isolated phrases hanging in the air. UBC still fourth among the Big Four . . . emphasis to shift away from programming to sales, at least at the top. . . . "You sell as regularly and naturally as other people pee, Matthew." He, Benning, could now give all his attention to programming, he was bringing in Gundelman from ABC to help him in this chore . . . "As you can see, a pretty sweeping reorganization." He patted the arm of his chair. "Hell of a hot seat to sit in, but the consensus is you're a hell of a hot man."

His voice stopped and an immense silence filled the office. Matthew tried to move his mouth, to speak, and couldn't. All he managed was a sort of convulsive click.

Benning gazed at him in mild alarm. "Hey, pal, relax. You're not concealing a tricky heart or anything under that vest, are you? Your color is—"

The cork that was Matthew hurtled itself out of the drowning crashing wave and bobbed to the surface.

"Just stunned," he said. "Overcome. Flabbergasted. And to continue, pleasantly surprised."

"Well, good. Wine, women, and jets do take it out of you." Benning went to a wall cabinet and took out a bottle of scotch and two glasses. "A little malt ought to restore you." Pouring, he added, "I wouldn't have told you unless it was a ninety-nine per cent sure thing. We won't show our hand until—let's see, to-day's Thursday—Monday. Just one more dear old thing's hearing aid to be talked into, and you're in like Flynn." They both drank, quickly and neatly. "And now if I were you I'd get on home, or to some restful bower anyway, and pull myself together."

He was still, for a last few days, president; he could still dismiss with authority and finality. He reached out a tanned hand and gave Matthew his famous firm grasp. "It couldn't happen to a better guy. Love to Joy."

A man in a dream, his legs still uncertain under him, Matthew took the express elevator forty-eight floors down. Expecting, as he had, to be away for a week, he had cleared his calendar of immediate matters to be dealt with. There was no reason not to walk out into the April sunlight; to play hooky from school.

Particularly when so soon he himself would be sitting in the principal's office.

For a bad moment he was afraid he was going to burst into tears of boundless relief, right here on East Fifty-sixth Street. He hastily hailed a cab, got in, and then couldn't think what directive to give.

Joy would be at work, and he didn't want to give her the news over the telephone. He wanted to see her face when he told her.

A glance at his watch—it was only ten thirty now. One half hour, and only a few minutes of it the operative ones, to snatch him back from the edge of a sort of grave.

To the driver, he said, "The Metropolitan Museum."

He needed a place to be quiet, a place to think and recover himself. Because after getting in he found there were two Matthews on the badly sprung seat of the cab.

One was the triumphant president-to-be of UBC, feeling as if he had swallowed not two fingers of Haig & Haig but a bucket of icy-simmering champagne. The unforeseen and impossible dropped in his lap, the rainbow's end reached, showering pink and golden and green and lavender light all over him.

That poor little Lloyd boy, dreadful about his father—d'you think young Bobby's clothes will fit him? I'm told they haven't a red cent—

President.

The other Matthew, eerily present at his side, was the cowering vomiting man crowding the ruined rest of a lifetime into five hours on the American Airlines jet. The engines singing "Nellie, Nellie." And the final, pre-New York drifting, falling, into an uneasy hot half-sleep. The jet engines taking up a different tune. "You've coped before," they sang from some remote humming distance. "You've coped before, Matthew. You've . . . coped . . . before . . ."

The Matthew next to the window in the taxi, gulping air: "But now everything's changed. How, not to put too fine a point upon it, magnificent."

The Matthew to his left: "*But.* You will have so much more to lose."

Nine

When she arrived at Babylon at two o'clock Thursday, Lukie Callender had added another uncharacteristic element to her disguise: fear.

She came in panting. Her Titian hair was wild. Inside the door, her long daisy-strewn skirt swayed as though a wind was still blowing through it.

What now? Nellie wondered wearily. "Yes," she said to her customer, "I do like the green on you a bit better than the blue. But still, the blue, there's something . . . it might be a good idea to take both."

"I will, you extravagant woman," her customer said. "And now that you're spending all of my money for me, that ten-foot rope of pearls in the window. How Enid has the nerve to charge twenty-five dollars for it, but she has to live, I suppose. You can put everything in one of those nice mattress-ticking shopping bags. I don't suppose you'd just throw it in?"

Nellie smiled. "Enid has to live." The departing customer emptied the shop. Not really wanting to hear Lukie's troubles, she asked, however, "What's wrong, Lulu?" She had called Lukie's number last night to tell her about the bleached boy and in a way was relieved when there was no answer; she found herself not wanting to think about him. A casual and possibly dangerous encounter that as a New Yorker you had to learn to live with. Dismiss it.

But still, one had responsibilities. "Before you tell me, there's something I should tell you."

Gradually recovering her breath, Lukie listened. Her mouth corners dented grimly in a fleeting *I thought so* expression. "There may or may not be a connection," she said, "but I've been ransacked, have I *ever* been ransacked!"

She had, she said, slept late this morning. She woke at twelve and found that there was nothing to eat. Too hungry to bother to put on all that crazy makeup right away, she had gone downstairs and around the corner to Maria's coffee-wine shop on Bleecker Street. She was pleased to find other late-breakfasting friends there and spent an hour over her English muffins and coffee and pizza and burgundy.

Going back up to don her armor, she found the door to her apartment slightly open. She called out, "Hey, who's there?" and took a tighter grip on the strap of her shoulder bag. The borrowed gun in it felt reassuring, pressing against her ribs. Silence.

She pushed the door open to chaos. The apartment was never tidy to begin with but now it looked as though a highly localized tornado had hit it. Furniture overturned, everything slashable knifed and torn; drawers wrenched out. The brutal combination of thoroughness and carelessness about it hit her hard. Junk furniture, picked up off the street or at the Salvation Army, but still — It felt as though large ruthless feet had trampled all over her own body.

Okay, it could have been anyone doing it to anybody. There was no television set or radio or stereo stuff to steal, she didn't own any of those things. There was no time for them; she seldom came home before two or three in the morning and when she did she fell into a bottomless sleep. Or at least she did when she was alone.

She found herself wishing that Dean and his State Department hadn't left town last night for an engagement in Philadelphia. Private party, she forgot whose name, and then they'd be going on to Atlantic City, gloriously open for anyone who wanted to pick up some money, any kind of money. She had no idea how long they'd be working in Atlantic City. No Dean, at least for the time, to rely upon, to flee to.

It was almost a comforting thought that the apartment above, Peter's, had been broken into last week, cleaned out of the quickly saleable things she didn't possess, and for bad luck an heirloom Chippendale mirror furiously smashed. Thank God she had no heirlooms, nothing of value, just herself and—

She clasped the shoulder bag against her side again. Telling a distressed-looking Nellie, she left this part out.

She would long since have put the money in the bank but she had a bone-deep distrust of all authority. Who knows, some stool pigeon of a banker, informed about the deposit of thirty thousand dollars in cash by a girl who couldn't be much more than twenty, might in turn inform the police. Well, not quite the original amount; she had dipped into it on occasion, at first intending to replace it.

Until she heard on the grapevine that Tost was out of prison, she had kept the money in a rosebud-patterned chipped china covered dish in her refrigerator. Any hungry marauder lifting the lid would merely see an inner little tray kept filled with moldy raspberry Jello. For the past few days, she had carried a thick white envelope around with her, snuggled in the bottom of the huge leather bag with the gun to keep it company.

"No, they didn't take anything, there was nothing really to take. Used clothes—forget it."

Tost knew where she lived, to say the least. She couldn't go back there, or certainly not tonight, back to the savage slashes, bleeding tufts of cotton, and twanging springs.

Enid's place wouldn't do. It would be the natural thing to look for her at her aunt's, if she turned out not to be with any of her friends.

"Not to leap to conclusions," Nellie said, "could it have been that odd-looking boy who was asking for you this morning?"

Her fear of him was obvious. Lukie said quickly, "No, the character that this is all about"—she flicked her hand at her face and hair—"and who may have done it, is very dark. Spanish-looking. Anyway, a cheap crook doesn't have to be a friend of yours to tear your place to pieces. Can I, dear Nellie, stay with you tonight? Please? My mattress is wrecked, even. I'll have to buy a new one and I'm on late tonight . . ."

Nellie hesitated. It seemed to her a bit foolhardy to say yes, and cruel to say no. If something happened to the girl because she was denied shelter she would never forgive herself. Besides, safety in numbers . . . and there was Titania.

Safety. Company for her, in the silent apartment on a noisy street.

In a last feeble effort to extricate herself from Lukie and her dubious circle, she protested, "But you've already told someone you're staying with me. Won't he, or they, or whoever—?"

With a logic and trust quite unlike her normal approach to others, Lukie said, "Yes, a bit of dust in the eyes, sorry you were bothered—but you told him I wasn't there, so naturally he'll go looking for me elsewhere. Probably only wanted to hit me for a loan or something."

That, she thought to herself, was rich. Hit me for a loan. A little matter of almost thirty thousand. In the two years he had been away, she had come increasingly to think of it as more or less hers. Ill-gotten gains didn't really belong to anybody but the particular person who happened to have their hands on them, was her way of putting it.

And you never knew when you'd want to cut out. And what a lovely launching pad the money made.

He'd want more than the money, he might want her back too, and she'd outgrown people like Tost, who from this distance of time looked like a crazy kind of rackety boy to get yourself mixed up with.

Dean ought to be back soon, Dean would take care of her when and if she could no longer take care of herself. Just walk a tightrope until his return. Or if things got really scary, skip for a while.

"All right," Nellie said. "But just the one night." She searched for a lie. Whom could she be expecting tomorrow night? Lukie saved her the trouble.

"I'll find another place tomorrow, I haven't got a lease at this dump and I honestly don't think I could sleep in peace there ever again."

"You notified the police, of course?"

"No, I didn't want to hang around there. I stuffed some things in my bag and ran around to Maria's and changed and fixed my face in the ladies'. Peter brought me over here on his motorcycle. But I will later, notify them, I mean," Lukie ended mendaciously, thinking, Who wants their name on *their* blotters?

The occasionally endearing girl hidden behind the makeup and deep inside the standard rebel of her generation showed herself in a charming three-cornered grin.

"You are a love, Nellie. No wonder everybody robs you blind.

Of kind good deeds in your case," and Nellie was warmly and swiftly hugged.

At four o'clock, Mr. Jove came into Babylon, thoughtfully eyed a green satin pants suit, said, "It might do for Mrs. Jove. The new one," to Enid, and then asked where Miss Hand might be.

He was a black man who did a brisk trade in the Village with his ever-ready pickup truck. He was slender, handsome, ageless, and almost never seen without his navy-blue beret worn with a Gallic insouciance. He provided for his customers, along with his truck, a bottomless pit of information about everybody, if they cared to ask. And if he chose to tell.

He and Enid were old friends. He liked baseball and she was, in his words, out of her mind about it. They occasionally shared, in front of her television set, a bottle of sour-mash Bourbon during the World Series, or at tense deciding games leading up to it.

Enid now exchanged a few bits of daily gossip with him. He admired her, a don't-give-a-damn kind of woman, a lady though. Tall, thin, looked at you when she was really interested through her lorgnette rimmed and handled with gold and held halfway down her beautiful long nose over her derisive mouth. Not a devotee of the moderately priced clothes she sold, she wore a thirteen-year-old black silk linen Norell, a flawless garment not so much sewn as carved.

"I was just passing this horrible *vulgar* new bath shop up the street," Enid said to him, placing a cigarette in her long scarlet holder. "I don't know what the neighborhood's coming to. It struck me that the world resolves itself into two kinds of people, the ones who have toilet seat covers or would like to, and the ones who do not and will not have them."

Jove took a second look at the green satin suit. "I suppose it might be marked down sooner or later— Yes, I take your meaning, Enid. But where was I? Asking for Miss Hand."

"She's pinning up a skirt in one of the dressing rooms." Enid raised her voice, cracked creamy finishing-school sound. "Nellie! Jove's here—and I forgot to tell you. The most amazing thing. I went up to have lunch with Jennifer—you remember her, the girl whose infant the father stole from your apartment a year or so ago—and what do you think?"

"What?" asked a dim voice from behind the apple-green canvas curtain.

"It's a small world. One thinks of these big executives as being so busy all day and half the night. But whom should I see, his back I mean, but Matthew Jones striding up the stairs of the Metropolitan."

There was another small, softer, "What . . . ?" from the dressing booth.

"Yes, it had to be Matthew. In spite of the however many million we live with now, no one else is so pink and so black and so well-tailored," Enid said. "And I may add that he had the stance of a Roman emperor. He must have gotten another underarms client. Or perhaps loose dentures. Until she's finished pinning, Jove, come along to the office, we'll let Lukie cope. It will take her mind off being burgled, poor dear."

Jove, it turned out, had come for Nellie's key. He had Mrs. Lyle's desk in his truck.

"I don't know, I have only the one key," Nellie said, sounding vague and looking pale and unlike her cheerful accommodating self.

"You might as well go with him," Enid said. Nellie hesitated, wondering if it was wise to leave the shop at all, wondering if she could face being left alone in her apartment.

Why was he back after just two days, when he was to be away for a week?

And no call, not even a simple local New York call. Hi Nellie, bad penny's turned up sooner than expected.

An unbelieving sort of relief threatened the stability of her knees. Perhaps—yes—it was just exactly as simple as it had seemed at first: he trusted her. Ignominious to think that that had become far more important, right now, than what he trusted her *about*.

Under Enid's penetrating eye, she retrieved her normal rosiness and without being aware of it let out a long sighing gasp.

"Thank you, Enid. I'll pay you back the hour and forty-five minutes one fine day."

"Don't count your chickens," Enid said.

Ten

"Get out of here!" shouted Lise. "Get out, get *out!*"

The room still rang with their quarrel; or rather, her half of it. Gretel seldom raised her voice, which somehow made it even worse.

She looked enough like Lise to be recognized as her sister, but around her cradle the good fairies, making up for a bad job on Lise, had given her pink and cream coloring and shining honey-colored hair, now discreetly tinted to stay that way. Her tall body was going a little to fat and under the rose tweed suit a keen observer could sense the no-nonsense all-in-one which gave her, sitting or standing, a look of rigidity.

"How you can bear all those strappings is beyond me," thin Lise would cry. "If there really was a heaven and hell you'd go straight on up, you're having your hell right here inside all that *elastic*. Boned too, no doubt."

Gretel picked up her thin leather gloves. "As I have said what I wished to say, for the moment, yes, I will leave you." But, not a woman of few words, she said it again, at the door.

"You will of course reconsider this ridiculous will. Bitterness and malice are bad for you, Lise, like drinking hemlock—might even speed your . . . I beg you to think of your family, your sister, your little nephews." She didn't mention her husband Robert. His and Lise's mutual dislike was irreversible. "You say two years, or three, but it could happen at any time, too late for you to correct what's really only one of your gestures."

"How practical you are, as always," Lise snarled. "I'm still strong enough to throw you out." She sat up on her sofa and Gretel went in her dignified rigid way out the door, closing it quietly, reprimandingly, behind her. The absence of a slam said,

I'm in control of myself, even if you've gone off the rails, you madwoman.

Gretel walked west on Eighth Street, disapproving everything that met her eye. Horrible tatty place, the Village. She'd tried for years to get Lise to move. A nice little garden apartment, near her family or what was left of it, in East Orange. Such a pleasure for her to be able to see the children once or twice a week. Although she said she didn't like children, they bored her. But yes, a clean sunny little place, geraniums on the window-sills, a decent kitchen.

Today, trying to bottle up her own rage or at least funnel it constructively, hadn't seemed a good day to press the East Orange move.

In one way or another, this thing had to be stopped.

There was a down-at-heels-looking pickup truck parked in front of 20 Timothy Street. Gretel, pausing, frowned at the faded blue canopy right across from it, some horrible place called the Evil Hour. A tall redheaded boy in an apron, leaning on his broom, stood under the canopy. He looked at Gretel and called, "You're too early for us, mother. We don't open until eight." He grinned gleefully.

The front door of No. 20 was open. Honestly, the way these people lived, an invitation to thugs, burglars, anyone could just walk in. Steal everything you owned, murder you in your bed—

Basil Perov came out of the hall door of his gallery. "Yes?" he asked. "Looking for someone?"

You never could tell from these people's clothes. "Are you the landlord? Or the superintendent? In what apartment can I find a Miss Nellie, Helen I suppose, Hand?"

Basil ticketed her immediately. Close connection of Lise Kozer's, same mouth and nose, but formidable in a way temperamental Lise never was.

He gave her the apartment number and watched as with a straight back she tackled the stairs.

She met the desk, blocking her now panting progress, halfway between the second and third floors. Mr. Jove was carrying it up sideways and had stopped to rest against the wall.

"Would you mind getting that thing out of the way? I'm in rather a hurry."

He took out a handkerchief and wiped his forehead. He smiled amiably at her. "Heart. Can't be hurried. Wants to get its breath back."

Gretel glared at him and then at the desk. It was white and slender-legged. Some talented amateur had painted ivy up the legs, cornflowers and poppies on the writing surface. There was a broad deep front drawer decorated with forget-me-nots, and at the back were six shallow drawers flowered to match. Above them, the desk decided it might possibly serve as a dressing table too, with a hinged three-way gilt-framed mirror. In the center of each beveled glass was painted a luxuriant butterfly.

"Can't you possibly lift it *up* a few stairs and let me by?"

"When the heart says okay I will. It wants a minute or so more," Jove explained, watching the pink-cheeked face turn more so with frustration and rage. He thought accurately, I'll bet she'd love to shove back the clock and give me a taste of the cat-o'-nine-tails.

From above, a voice called, "Need any help? The last flight is the hardest."

"No, just about home free now." He moved and Gretel of necessity climbed slowly after him.

"Just inside the door will do, Jove," Nellie said. "There. That's fine." She put a folded bill into his shirt pocket.

"You shouldn't do that. Mrs. Lyle's already paid me *and* tipped me for the stairs. Thanks though."

In all the twenty years Nellie had known Lise, she had met Gretel just twice. The last time had been five years ago. She said, "Gretel. Were you looking for me?"

"I don't climb four flights of stairs just for the exercise," Gretel said indignantly. "Yes, we must have a talk."

She walked uninvited into Nellie's hall, went into the living room, and sat firmly on the slipper chair.

"I've just left Lise. I won't waste my time or yours. You can't mean to tell me you really intend to suck the blood of a dying woman." It was a statement, not a question.

The cold wave of hostility struck Nellie hard. She didn't, somehow, want to sit in this woman's presence. Sitting down, you were too vulnerable.

"What are you talking about?"

"What am I talking about?" A kind of inner corseting holding Gretel together seemed to snap. "Your expectations, I hope you know it, are a joke. You're a joke. A whim of Lise's. Enid was there before you, we had Enid as heir pushed in our faces for several years. And then it was a home for abandoned cats in Morrisania, in the Bronx. And now, you."

Nellie felt behind the facade of this tweed-suited suburban matron an old and basic savagery. People, she thought, will say anything for money. Do anything for money.

What money?

She was outraged and she groped for words. Sucking the blood of . . .

"Is it the Royal Worcester egg coddler you're talking about? Or this?" She held out her wrist, on it a thin silver bracelet with a tiny turquoise frog making the clasp. Lise had said, "It was my mother's, you must have it for your birthday."

"Don't play absentminded old maid games with me," Gretel said. She got up and moved to face Nellie, in her hand her heavy expensive crocodile bag.

I thought they'd stopped killing crocodiles long ago, crossed Nellie's mind, I thought it was against the law.

"I'd say call her right now but she'd know I'd come over here and might call the police. She's that crazy. No. Go sit down with a pen and a piece of paper and write that you cannot accept being her heir, she's temporarily out of her mind. You're very grateful to her but—but you realize her responsibilities to her family."

An ugly dream. But Gretel was there, two feet from her, beginning to swing the crocodile bag. A fleeting awful memory from some book she'd read came to Nellie, Greek guerrillas during an internecine war, the ghastly things they did, swooping down from the hills, to men, women, and children.

Gretel fixed her with hypnotizing cold furious eyes. "Go ahead. *Now*. We'd take you to court in any case, you haven't a prayer, but it's easier for everybody this way."

"That monster, that beast," came clearly back to Nellie. A single-minded woman, selfish, powerful, and determined, perhaps one of the most dangerous of all living creatures.

Echoing this, Gretel said softly, harshly, "It's not only me, it's my children, my father's, my mother's grandchildren. It's my family. It's mine. She's no good to anybody any more. Except to us. She'd never forgive herself, leaving it to any"—a ferocious grin that was like and unlike Lise, a good deal more frightening, on the apple-round face—"Nellie, Dick, or Harry. I believe her brain's gone. She went on and on about your cabbage soup. I think she was planning to pay you a very high price indeed for —among other casual kindnesses—your cabbage soup."

As though deliberately, she lost control. Her arm went up and she swung the bag high over her head. It came down and smacked her substantial thigh, a noise as frightening and explicit as a pistol shot.

"Leave my apartment," Nellie said, her voice with that breathless squeak when physical fear caught her, like, she had often thought, a maddened mouse. "Or *I* will call the police."

Gretel tossed her weapon, her handbag, onto the sofa and grasped Nellie's shoulders with fingers that bit in.

"Pen and paper, I said. Right now."

Going down the stairs, Jove had stopped to knock at Ursula's door. She opened it with the politely annoyed look of somebody interrupted at an absorbing moment.

"Woman, big get-out-of-my-way woman, just came to see Miss Hand. Walked right in past her without a by-your-leave, looks like she's looking for trouble. You might keep an ear open."

Ursula had never thought about it before, but now realized that Nellie was one of her private Gibraltars. A survivor. A doughty woman who could walk through fire and flood and come out unscathed. Someone you leaned against, confided in, dried your tears in front of, not someone herself in need of help.

"Okay," she said. "I'll run up in a couple of minutes."

On cue with Gretel's pen-and-paper demand, she ran up the stairs. The door was an inch or so open. Ordinarily a graceful, mannerly sort of girl, she charged into Nellie's living room like a field-hockey player. "Hi!" she cried merrily. "I'm here!"

Gretel took her hands off Nellie's shoulders. "Would you mind? We are having a private interview."

"On my agenda, it's our teatime," Ursula said, returning cheerful obtuseness for rudeness. "I'll make it, Nellie. And right after,

you know, you promised to pose for me. I won't let you off no
matter what."

"Just the sort of behavior I would have expected of Lise's
friends." Gretel opened her bag and presented Nellie with her
card. "Here is my address. I'll expect the letter from you, or
rather a copy of the one you are to send to Lise, no later than
Monday. Otherwise we will take steps."

To the soft closing of the door behind her, Nellie said, "Thank
you, Ursula."

"What was she planning to do, throw you out the window?"

Nellie explained, and sighed. ". . . and if poor Lise applied
for welfare payments she could probably get them hands down.
She has little enough to amuse her, I suppose her will is something she plays with, a kind of toy. But then you've heard all
about the famous fortune. Everybody has."

"All the way out to East Orange," Ursula said, studying the
engraved card. "But if I were you, Nellie, I wouldn't make an
appointment for my next interview with her in a dark alley."

Jeremy Orr, by nature a walker, found himself heading downtown on Lexington Avenue. The April day had turned gray and
chilly. The wind was sharply refreshing after a four-hour session
in the studio, doing three color shots for ads for Melinda Rum.
There had been a bad moment when a model, waiting for the
next shot, had lifted a glass from a cluttered table to the left of
the camera and raised it thirstily to her lips.

It had been used an hour before, in a close-up of a drink
called a Melinda Mist. The heat of the lights precluded the use
of ice and the rum when poured and lit looked too pale, wrong
color. The glass contained splintered glass, iodine, and water.
"Good Christ *no!*" Jeremy shouted just in time. The model
pouted. "Stingy thing." He had poured a small, real rum for both
of them. "Just to celebrate your still being in the land of the living. Sometimes I think I'd be well qualified to run a day-care
center."

In front of the Lexington Florists, a pre-Easter display of
flowering bulbs glowed. He lowered his nose to sniff a pot of
narcissus. Bending, bowing, but not breaking in the inclement
wind, snapping fragrantly back up again, green and white, deli-

cate and tough—now, who did the narcissus remind him of? It
tickled at the edge of his mind and then assumed identification:
Ursula Winter.

He went back two blocks and into the florists', and bought
two dozen cut narcissus. Bearing them in their thin silky green
paper wrapping, he thought he'd just have time to deliver them
and say hello to his aunt. He had been feeling vaguely guilty
about her since yesterday, remembering the astonished slapped
look on her face when he had barked at her, "What the *hell—*"

Peggy had administered a mild scolding later in the day. "I
mean you were *really*. A better temper normally I wouldn't look
for. But that poor woman was on some kind of brink. If I ever."

Himself an enemy of droppers-in, for whom he kept an imagi-
nary supply of poisoned arrows, he stopped at a phone booth
on lower Fifth Avenue and called Nellie's number; her hours at
Babylon were occasionally eccentric.

Buoyant light voice, whose? Yes, of course, Ursula's. "She's in
the shower washing her hair. Can she call you back?"

Nellie had asked after two cups of tea and the drink of scotch
that Ursula insisted she have, "Would you mind holding the fort
for ten or fifteen minutes while I wash my hair? In case she . . ."
stopping, looking abstracted and drawn, "or anyone . . ."

Ursula wondered if the fair pink shoulder-grasping woman
had done this to her. Tired, wilting; some loss of spine, of vigor.

On another plane, she wondered if Jeremy thought she spent
the better part of twenty-four hours a day at Nellie's hoping for
the sight or at least the sound of him.

God, he would think, there's that girl *again*.

"Will you tell her I'll be there in seven minutes?"

"Yes," Ursula said, and before she could stop herself, "She
needs you."

She opened the bathroom door and gave the message to billowing water-rushing shower curtains. "I'll stay till he gets here,
shall I? Don't skimp your rinsing, Nellie, no hurry."

And then our two ships, thank you, will pass very swiftly in
the night, at the door of 4B.

Nellie did hurry with her hair and came out damp and robed.
Her wet hair, combed close against her head, made her face look
thinner, less open and dimply. She had put her lipstick on crook-

edly—hands shaking after Gretel's visit?—and had made feverish inefficient use of her powdered blusher.

"You'll stay, Ursula?" as the doorbell rang.

"No, must run. Hello, Jeremy."

"Hello, Ursula. Don't go." Carrying his flowers, trench coat open, he looked windy and dark and fresh; and seemed to be studying her face as if to see whether he had got it right.

He pulled out one of the narcissus and gave it to her. "For behind your ear or between your teeth or wherever it suits you."

Their eyes met in a brief startling crash.

"Much obliged," Ursula said, and from the doorway, "Thank you for the tea, Nellie."

"Thank *you*, more than I can say."

Jeremy kissed her cheek and went into the kitchen to put the flowers in water. When he came back, Nellie was fumblingly trying to make a fire with the last of her apple logs. "Might as well burn them up now it's spring. I'm cold, are you?"

"Not at all, but let me do that." Everything he did with his hands always went swiftly, faultlessly. The kindling caught and a flame curled yellow around a small log. He had been dividing his close attention between his fire and her face.

He came and sat down on the sofa beside her. "What's wrong, Nellie?"

As always with those bearing heavy burdens silently, close loving sympathy was a dangerous picker of locks.

Don't, don't. *Don't.*

There were tears in her eyes. "Just three sort of . . . peculiar upsetting things in a row." Talk, talk yourself away from the first of these things, Matthew. "But of course at this time last year there was that boy who was going to commit suicide every night at six, and called me at a quarter of. You remember, it went on for a week. And Lise not able to get home alone from her cooking classes because she'd eaten what she'd cooked and was frightfully ill . . . I suppose after a ghastly winter, spring does strange things to people. Yesterday I almost—when I went running like an idiot to your studio—mistook a boy here, looking for a friend of his, for a hired executioner or something like that—"

Had she really conceived this idea about the boy, somewhere

in the recesses of her mind? Had she dreamed it, about him? The words had not until this moment shaped themselves.

No. Just as she had said, three peculiar things, after all nothing new in her life.

Matthew's story, which obviously she didn't have to worry about any more. From a personal, physical point of view.

A boy looking for Lukie, magnified into a monster because the pigmentation of his skin was a little abnormal.

Lise's sister Gretel, obsessed as Lise was with the legendary family money. Obsessions induced erratic behavior. Ignore the whole matter, dismiss it.

The burglary attempt at Lukie's apartment was a fourth thing, but that was a commonplace and unconnected with her, Nellie.

"What am I thinking of, I'll get you a drink." The tears, which she hadn't been aware of, had made little runnels down her cheeks.

"I'll do it." He was back in under a minute. "I have to go soon, Nellie. But whatever it is, tell me. Right now." He put a thin strong hand on her wrist and tightened it comfortably. He felt an obscure alarm. Hired executioner. Woe, on the firelit, unquenchably young and innocent face. Where had staunch Nellie gone, and who was this woman she had left behind in her place? Dithering. Nellie never dithered.

He sensed that in some fashion Ursula had been just now taking care of his aunt and he wanted to know why.

"There is absolutely nothing you can't tell me, Nellie," he said, gently and insistently.

Well . . . yes. Or is it just that I'm so tired and he's so dear, Nellie thought.

She put the back of her hand to her forehead. "First too cold and now too hot. Matthew . . ."

Was she glad or sorry when the telephone rang? She wasn't sure.

It was Charmian. "The painters are coming tomorrow. May I take shelter in your place? I know I have a key somewhere."

"If you can't find it call me before nine thirty. There's a new Ngaio Marsh I haven't started yet."

"Lovely." Voice purring and blooming. "What would we all do without you," said Charmian.

Turning from the telephone, she said, "That was Charmian." In a last-ditch effort to pull back, divert his attention, so warm, so penetrating, she added, "I'm afraid she's fallen in love."

He felt oddly relieved. Nellie did get involved in other people's emotions, crises; in a way lived vicariously through them.

"Is that, then, one of your peculiar things? I'd say it was Walter Lyle's worry, not yours."

He looked at his watch. "Promise to call me. Next time you're cold and"—he kissed her cheek again—"almost in tears."

"I will, Jeremy dear." Hurry away, Jeremy. Hurry. Before Matthew invisibly catches up with both of us. And makes me tell.

Lukie kept her word for practical reasons and arrived at 20 Timothy Street right after Babylon's ten o'clock closing. She gave the three short rings and one long one Nellie had asked her for. She was a girl well used to signals. The door was opened, her hostess for the night covering a yawn.

"Stay up as long as you like. You won't go out and come back in, will you? Titania"—hand reassuringly on the afghan's head as the stranger entered—"would raise the roof. Help yourself to whatever you want from the refrigerator. I'm in bed with a book."

The sofa in the living room was already made up, clean and crisp if not coordinated. A striped sheet doubled, a flowered pillowcase on the squashy pillow, a bandana-patterned cotton quilt ready at the foot. The fire was out but the apartment smelled of consumed warm fragrant wood.

"I can't thank you enough," Lukie said. "I've got a place with a friend for the next few days so it'll be only for this one night. Go back to bed. Shall I bring you hot milk or something?" She had a dim remembrance of an Aunt Claire who always partook of this beverage before retiring.

"No thanks, I'm all but asleep."

Good.

Lukie listened for a while to a rock station on her transistor radio, turned down to a jarring whisper. Then she checked locks and latches in a businesslike way, washed her face, and brushed her teeth.

Just before she got in between the halves of the striped sheet, she strolled the living room speculatively, went into the hall, and stood contemplating the pretty white desk.

She opened the long deep front drawer. It was full of stuff. Letters, mismatched gloves, scrambled-up costume jewelry, some kind of books all alike with ivory leather bindings scattered with gold bees. About the drawer's contents, she was incurious. With two fingers, she lifted a pile and slid under it the thick white envelope from her shoulder bag.

In her mind, she said gratefully, "Well. One thing off my back."

Eleven

See her or don't see her?

Matthew battled with it until Saturday evening. He badly wanted to know what her attitude to him was now, to take her emotional pulse.

It might just sting awake recollections she had already begun to store safely away, turn her back on. Seeing him in the flesh, his face, his hands—"I got his neck in my hands"—might make the whole thing real in a fresh and unbearable way.

Look upon me, look upon death.

But the temptation left him not a moment's peace. It shadowed for him Joy's delight, as, sparkling, she flung her arms around him. "My husband the president!" It was with him when he woke in the predawn hours, impatiently underwent fittings for several new suits, called a few close friends with his news. "Not official yet. Wish me luck though."

It was like wondering, when you left the apartment for a weekend, if the gas cocks on the stove had been turned firmly off or if one of them was awry and still breathing. And whether, fumes slowly but surely circulating, spontaneous combustion— the apartment might blow up. You knew, you were certain, that you had checked—you always did—but what if this time you hadn't? You went reluctantly back, cursing yourself, to find that of course the gas was safely off.

He didn't dare admit to himself that he wanted more than the assurance of silence. He wanted understanding and sympathy for the burden he carried. He wanted, more important from her than from anybody else, congratulations on bounding right up to the top.

The new job, why not? She'd be hurt if she found out about it weeks later, heard it from someone else. It was the least he could do to let her be among the first to know. Tell her, in fact, that she was the first.

Joy had a dinner conference with board members of one of her clients, Worldways Business Machines. "I hate to leave you in your hour of triumph, Matthew. Shall I get a steak out of the freezer or will you go out?"

Matthew decided not to call Nellie beforehand. He wanted to take her by surprise, see the unprepared face before caution or good manners hid what he must find, must see.

He pressed Ursula's buzzer button. When the hollowed distorted voice asked who it was he said, "Matthew. Hit yours by mistake but I might drop by and say hello."

By the third flight, he was reaching for breath. Must get into better shape, and fast. Look at Benning. But then on the other hand look what had happened to Benning. Promoted into a soundless vacuum from which, probably, he would be no more heard.

He knocked lightly at Nellie's door. He heard a floorboard creak, then felt the listening silence very near him.

This wouldn't do. He didn't know her domestic habits, how likely or unlikely she was to answer an unbuzzed-for knock.

"Nellie? It's Matthew."

It was three or four seconds before the door was opened. What was she doing, looking into the hall mirror, fixing her hair? Or had she whipped into the bedroom to change a garment not suitable for receiving visitors in? Or, perhaps calming a thunder of the heart?

"He*llo*, Matthew," Nellie, not Nellie at all, said. "Won't you come in? I'm dressed for reading, please excuse it." Woolly pink robe—the night was cold and rainy and her heat was never quite adequate—pink slippers, pale face, hands thrust into the robe pockets. Clenched?

"Excuse *me* for just bursting in. I had to see you and tell you before anyone else. Something wonderful's happened." He hugged her and deliberately willed himself back to Matthew-before-Tuesday-night, big jovial confident Matthew.

Nellie didn't detach herself but waited mutely until he dropped his arms. "Well, then. Come on in. Your coat is soaking, I'll hang it over the bathtub. I'm afraid I burned up all my logs the other night, the last of them, and with this nasty rain coming down— But I can offer interior warmth, especially as you say there's something to celebrate . . ."

They were both aware that she was talking too much and too fast. Oh God, Matthew thought. But it doesn't *mean* anything, merely that she's naturally just a little uncomfortable with me.

"Do sit down, while I—"

She found herself sorry that Titania's owner, having had a furious quarrel with her mother, had come back from Charleston sooner than expected and had collected her dog this afternoon.

"No, I'll come along and help. If only to unscrew the bottle cap."

Her kitchen gave him a sense of home, although it resembled none he had grown up with. Disorderly and at the same time immaculate: an unrinsed blue teapot thick with tea leaves in the sink, blue and white gingham curtains looped back above a broad sill from which George the cat, nestled against a clay pot of marguerites, gave him an inquiring green glare. A smell of roses, no, not roses, good English tea. Instead of grim fluorescents overhead, a lamp made out of a wine bottle, with a glowing geranium red shade, on one corner of the counter, warm and rich as the fire Nellie was unable to provide.

She opened the refrigerator door, reached in, and dropped the copper ice-cube tray on the floor. "Oh dear . . ."

He picked up the tray and gave the aluminum handle a hearty wrench, making the cubes leap into the air.

"Apparently I'm to be president of UBC, Nellie," he said, and wondered why his voice was so loud. Perhaps only because the kitchen was so small, and she was so near, and seeming to be shrinking away from him, against the counter.

The announcement sounded to him meaningless, frivolous, held alongside his other, recent communication. *"I killed him, Nellie, did you hear me? I choked him to death with my bare hands."*

Not looking at him, she handed two glasses. "Oh. How *marvelous.*" Faraway timbre, like Ursula through the buzzer sound system; not her eager birdsong response.

He poured scotch. "Yes. I was summoned back from the Coast. No explanation. I had no idea whether the skies were falling—"

He stopped and watched her pink wool back as she reached into the wall cabinet for a packet of salted sunflower seeds. She didn't turn her head when he left the statement hanging. The tendrils of hair against the nape of her neck, Matthew thought, were like a child's.

"But that's the way it is in this business. You always expect the worst. And leaving out business, the way I was brought up *I* always expect the worst. Nellie? Do turn around and see what a brand-new television network president looks like before he starts to turn a little scorched around the edges."

She did turn around, not daring to let him have the use and examination of her eyes. She looked at the marbled blue-and-white asphalt-tile floor and said, "If George would only not scatter his kibbles about. I mopped it this morning, believe it or not."

"Let's take these and sit down," Matthew said, picking up the two glasses. "It's time for quiet. And peace. I don't know how or why you've got yourself a corner on peace, Nellie, but I'd like to wallow in it for a while."

From the moment when she had opened the door, Nellie knew that this was the last time. That she couldn't see Matthew again, or know him any more. It wasn't a judgment but a simple re-action, recognition. Basic and final.

He clinked his glass against hers after they had sat down on the sofa. "Just this one, and then I'd like to take you out to dinner. Charles, I thought. As a matter of fact I made a reservation for two on the way here, for eight o'clock."

"Matthew, I can't . . ."

In the silence, George came in from the kitchen and jumped on the arm of the sofa. And a voice soared up from the street, "Yea verily I tell you, Christ has come again and will soon be among us."

"Oh heavens, John the Baptist shouldn't drink at all, but he only does on Saturdays," Nellie said desperately. "You've seen him? A goatskin, and leather straps sort of crisscrossed around his calves? But very nice, gentle . . ."

Matthew took a long gulp of his drink and set the glass down on the end table beside him. His eyes swiveled away from Nellie's face, circling the apartment. "Pretty desk you've got in the hall. Is that new?"

"No, on loan from Charmian, she hasn't room for it."

Matthew finished his drink. He put a long dark blue arm across the back of the sofa. His fingers touched the nape of her neck. She had the feeling of icicles dripping on the bare shuddering skin.

"Can't, Nellie? Can't go to dinner?" Matthew asked softly. "Or won't?"

She stumbled over an excuse. "I promised to pose for Ursula, robes for Mother's Day . . . even though I don't for better or worse look like anybody's mother. But she always works with a model of sorts, which is why her drawings look so—"

"Not even to celebrate the best thing that ever happened to me?" Matthew's eyes were close, and fiercely bright.

Leave out, in this royal progression, both of them thought, neither knowing the other's mind, the worst thing that ever happened to Roy Cox.

Matthew stood up, squaring his shoulders, settling the fit of his splendid double-breasted suit. Bending, he took her chin in his hand and looked, as it seemed to her, deep inside her head.

"Well, as we said when I was ten, all right for you, Nellie. And as the song goes . . . out in the rain again."

He gave her a kiss on her forehead that felt gentle and final.

After he had left, Nellie fought an aching throat. Don't start crying or you'll never stop. I need, I must have—

All she got was the answering service when she dialed Jeremy's house number.

"Any message?"

Yes, I'm lost and sad and soon I will be terrified. I don't know what these few last moments in this room meant.

"When do you expect Mr. Orr?"

"He left it a bit open," the girl said. "Monday or Tuesday and at the latest Wednesday. He's gone to, wait a minute, Scotland, I think to shoot a television commercial." Not knowing whether she was talking to a prospective client, "You're sure there's no message?"

"No, no message," said Nellie. And not wanting to be rude, added, to the answering service, "Good-bye."

Part Two

One

"Scotland," Jeremy mused after reading the script, a thirty-second television commercial for Corning's Bonnie Shortbread Cookies. "Couldn't it be done out at Montauk? It's their money, not mine, but still."

"The advertising manager probably wants an outing," Peggy Earl said. She finished typing up the bid, and frowned at the total. "We're sure to be the highest. Too bad. I do like Scotland."

Their bid was indeed the highest of the three submitted. Jeremy, in spite of this, got the assignment. "The things he does with light," the agency art director explained to the Corning advertising manager. "And of course with kids no one better. We'll do a new thing, flash a credit on the screen, he's a name, you know. You'll get picked up for that in the trade press."

The wrap-up cost of the commercial, including what was to come to Jeremy in large handfuls, was sixty-seven thousand dollars.

Still obscurely worried, he called his aunt Saturday morning from Kennedy before flying off. There was no answer. Too early for her to be on the way to work; she was probably doing her marketing, or had been snatched from her repose to attend upon someone's troubles.

Peggy was a superb organizer. She had telephoned ahead on Friday and arranged for the bagpipers, the elderly woman's voice over, and three girls of nine to ten, all with red hair, of whom one would be selected. The commercial was to be shot at Thisport, on St. Andrews Bay. In it, the little girl would be discovered by the camera at the water's edge in early morning, holding a conch shell to her ear. She would hear music, and in her waking dream bagpipers would come kilted up the strand. Then, from the shell she would hear and see wind whipping over high heather, firelight on a hearth, an oven door opening and the screech of a rack pulled out. "The bonnie taste of Scotland," murmured a strongly accented woman's voice from the shell, the voice of an ideal grandmother. "Taste the heather, taste the music of the pipers, taste the home fires of Scotland in Corning's Bonnie Shortbread Cookies." In the closing frames, a small hand would reach into a little straw basket with fresh daisies thrust through the handle, and help itself to the cookies.

The only thing Peggy could not organize was the weather. On Sunday it poured rain and everybody and everything expensively waited. Monday shone and the commercial was shot in eight hours, beginning at seven in the morning. Jeremy was effortlessly fast at his work, knowing beforehand exactly what he wanted to do.

Their plane landed at Kennedy at eight o'clock the following morning.

He called Nellie right after going through Customs. Again, no answer. In the unreal, nervous state that follows an Atlantic crossing, however smooth and punctuated with periods of sleep, he looked up Winter, Ursula, in the directory. She might be a late sleeper, but that was her hard luck.

"I can't seem to reach Nellie," he said when she answered. "Doesn't she ever stay home? I'm sorry if I waked you but—"

"She's—"

A silence which struck him like a thunderclap.

"She's what?"

"She was cremated yesterday afternoon," Ursula Winter said, or someone who sounded vaguely like Ursula Winter. And then, voice breaking, hoarse, "I'm terribly sorry, but I can't . . . they did try to reach you but you were in Scotland. Are you there now? Oh God . . ."

Another voice, Enid Callender's. "Everybody who loved her was there, yesterday," she said harshly. "Except those to whom the press of business is the first consideration."

"For Christ's sake, Enid," Jeremy managed. Peggy, standing a few feet away guarding their luggage, rushed over to him as he put a hand across his eyes. She took the receiver from him.

"Yes?" she said briskly. "We've just gotten in, we're at Kennedy. Is anything wrong?"

"Jeremy's aunt," Enid said slowly and carefully, "has been murdered. They think, the police, sometime Saturday night or early Sunday morning."

"He'll be more or less right there," Peggy said.

If he doesn't, she thought, crumple where he stands, my poor God-blessed Jeremy.

"I can't go home alone," Enid had said. "I believe I've never felt so alone in my life. May I stay with you, Ursula?"

It was she who came to the door of 3A. She gave him one look and said, "Brandy, I think. I'll join you." Ursula was nowhere in sight. What must be her bedroom door was closed.

"It was Ursula," Enid said, "who found her."

At around noon on Sunday, Ursula needed Nellie for her drawing of Mrs. Plumrose the Beekeeper in her *Buttercup Express.*

She ran up the stairs and as she lifted her hand to knock saw that the door was a little open. "Nellie?" she called.

No response. Perhaps she was in the bathroom. Not wanting to push her way in, Ursula went down the stairs, waited five minutes, and then dialed Nellie's number. She counted fifteen rings and then went back up again, and into the hall of 4B.

She registered the room beyond in a stopped shock of silence and immobility which might have lasted two seconds or two minutes.

Nellie lay face down on the shabby copper-rose Afghanistan rug, a great stain of blood covering the upper half of her pink wool robe.

Ursula heard her own half-scream, half-gasp. *"Nellie—"* Moving at last, she did the natural and forbidden thing: took Nellie's shoulder and pulled. She removed her hand almost instantly but not before she saw the face in profile, the eye half-open.

It was only later that she apprehended the whole scene, which her eyes had photographed with relentless clarity and which remained before her mental gaze down to the last sunlit dust motes as a curtain moved in the breeze at the open window.

The drawers of a chest pulled out, the handbag emptied on the floor beside the body, the scene of confusion visible through the open bedroom door. More yanked-open drawers, from one of which a pale blue slip dangled, sunlight catching the gleam of a small safety pin where the strap met the lace.

Unable to feel any emotion yet besides horror and revulsion, she ran down to her apartment and called the police. "Yes, she's dead, I think, I'm sure, the blood . . ."

The Sixth Precinct station house was nearby, on Tenth Street. In minutes she heard the siren and then deliberate feet on the stairway. She had been fumblingly looking for Jeremy's number, hampered by the fact that now her hands were shaking, and then her body, head to foot.

There was a crisp commanding knock at her door. The two uniformed men, one black, one white, identified themselves as Sergeants Lovell and Sundburg. "You're the Ursula Winter who placed the call?"

She made a tremendous and unsuccessful effort to stop the shaking. Through chattering teeth, she said, "Yes . . . but you won't need me, not up there, I mean? Not again—"

A mad thought struck her. So far they had no reason whatever to believe *she* hadn't done whatever terrible thing had happened to Nellie.

What, they would be thinking, was she doing up there anyway when she came across a so-called body.

Lovell was already up the next flight, and Sundburg, the black, said, "Come along, Miss," in a way that allowed no hanging back.

Lovell ended any remotely lingering doubt, or hope. "Yes. Dead," and still on one knee muttered into his walkie-talkie. With unexpected kindness gesturing toward the bedroom, Sundburg extracted from Ursula a preliminary statement, notebook and ball-point in hand.

She was, she said, a friend of the dead woman's, an old friend, a dear friend. She had gone up to get Nellie to pose for a drawing and found the door slightly open and after a bit had decided to go in.

She heard as she answered his questions new noises, voices, in the next room beyond the closed door. The usual ceremonies following upon sudden violent death, she supposed. Chalk marks on the rug to show how Nellie last lay, photographs, fingerprint dustings, the doctor who might in time do the autopsy, men with a stretcher, and something to cover it, cover Nellie, while they got the stretcher down the stairs, into the ambulance. Familiar details from books, from movies, but until now comfortably unreal.

Sundburg flipped over another page of his notebook. "You're not exactly underneath, but in old buildings like this— Did you hear anything at all last night from up above?"

"I was out until two. After that, no, I didn't hear a thing."

Sam, on the landing, had given every sign that it was the most important thing in life to go to bed with her immediately. She had known him for seven months and liked him very much; but she discovered, there outside her door, that at least until the year went its way and the earth took a turn, she didn't want anybody, unless it was Jeremy.

In the afternoon there was a ghastly gathering at her apartment, by anything but invitation. Basil and Lise, Enid and Charmian. Basil came in carrying a large bunch of white carnations.

"It's already all over our little world," he said. "Mr. Clean gave these to me at the door. For Nellie. Ursula, I'm not going to be polite, I brought my bottle along with the flowers and I'm about to avail myself of it."

He came back in with his glass. "Somebody's got to break the silence, it bangs on the eardrums. Well, flowers. Is there going to be all that barbaric business, Nellie all smoothed over and laid out, candles at her head and foot, chrysanthemums being foremost among the floral offerings because you get more bulk for less money?"

His abrasiveness was in a way healthy and helpful. In a room where for the time being there seemed nothing to say after their first horrified exchanges, he was walking squarely toward unfaceable things.

"No, none of that," Enid said, bright feverish color on cheeks that looked older, the fine skin sagging. "She left her will with me, she was always afraid of a fire and she didn't want to be bothered with a safe-deposit box. She specified cremation. From years back, I have her power of attorney, to pay bills or something when she was going on vacation, I forget what. She'll probably have money enough in the bank to cover it and if she doesn't we can manage among us." Blinking suddenly, she added, "I owe her two weeks' vacation pay."

"Shouldn't Jeremy be taking care of all this, I mean wouldn't he want to?" Charmian asked. "Where is Jeremy?"

Ursula explained that she had called and found he was on a job, in Scotland, on location, no telephone number where he could be reached left with his answering service; and that he was expected back early in the week.

"Tell me again," Lise said heavily. "I heard it but I didn't hear it, I pushed it all away. Ursula?"

Whitely, Ursula went over it. Her discovery of Nellie, the police, Enid summoned as Nellie's closest and oldest friend to see if she could say what, if anything, had been stolen. Enid's list of missing objects was pathetically brief: Nellie's mother's coral necklace, two rings of not much value, a watch that needed repairing and had been lying in her dresser drawer, her small portable black-and-white Sony television set, her wallet.

"But to *kill*," Lise said. "This slime usually only picks up what sticks to its fingers and runs."

"Nellie," Basil reminded her, "was a tough woman in her way. She might have put up a fight of some kind."

"I heard one policeman say that the way she was lying with her head toward her end table, she could have been reaching for the phone, either to call for help or to use for a weapon, the receiver I mean," Enid said. "Yes, Ursula, thank you," as Ursula handed her a strong measure of the Bourbon she kept especially for Enid's visits.

Charmian had been weeping on and off since she had arrived. The tears did not mar or twist her face but ran down in streams of crystal over her tight silky ivory skin. "I'll break my champagne rule for anything at all you have, Ursula. I know it happens up and down every street every day, the smash-and-grab . . . and last week there was an old woman killed, struck on the head, during a robbery on I think Bleecker Street. But in a way this seems like the end of the world. Does anybody think there's any chance they'll find out who did it? I don't."

"*If* they even look," Enid said tartly. "Of course, they'll go through the motions. But you know what floods into the Village on weekends, from the Bronx and Brooklyn and God knows where. To say nothing of our resident fly-boys. Knives by the hundreds in back pockets, I would assume. Look at what happened at Lukie's in broad daylight."

To save himself the trouble of trips to the kitchen, Basil brought in his bottle of vodka and set it at his elbow.

"There was that boy that Nellie was so frightened of, hanging around in the hall here the other day. I wish I'd gotten a look at him. Bleached, she said."

The police had questioned all the tenants of 20 Timothy Street and in the course of this had found that Timothy Liquors had made three deliveries Saturday night, the last one close to midnight; entrance by a person or persons bent on what might have been at first merely a burglary attempt wouldn't have been difficult. In addition, 2B had been moving out, and the door at the back of the hall was open for several hours while 2B transferred his goods and chattels into the U-Haul truck parked outside the door in the courtyard.

"I told them about the boy, and if you happen to stumble over anyone the description fits you might let them know." He repeated Nellie's impression of the boy. "Probably no connection, but"—with a savage gulp of his drink—"her friends owe her more than their attendance at her cremation. Tomorrow, Enid?"

"Tomorrow. The police say that they will be finished with . . . that they will release her body."

I can't bear them any longer, Ursula thought. I've got to get up and run. To whom? And then, in one of the brief flashes of memory-skip that follow upon shock, she thought, I'll just go upstairs and have a quiet cup of tea with Nellie.

"And that's about all anyone knows so far," Enid said. "In other words, nothing. Except a life snuffed out and a few trinkets taken. Business as usual at the same old stand."

This, Ursula told herself, this hiding in the bedroom is abject cowardice. It was just that for the time she couldn't bear to see his face.

She had heard very little of his voice: an occasional low question as Enid haltingly, unwillingly, proceeded with the account of his aunt's death.

Now, from the next room: "You're her heir. I suppose you'll

see to, or have someone see to, the contents of her apartment."

Trying to gather herself together, Ursula washed her face, brushed her hair, which when she was sad went curiously dank and seemed a darker, duller color, and opened the bedroom door.

Enid was digging in her crewel-embroidered shopping bag. She took out a cube-shaped box enameled in turquoise. "Here are her ashes. I didn't know if you'd want them or not."

Jeremy, sitting, shoulders bent, hands clasped between his knees, stared at the box, his eyes unnaturally large, like a child's eyes first facing something truly terrifying, paralyzing.

He reached out his hand and took the box and put it carefully on the floor beside him. "Did she ask"—voice formal, polite—"that they be scattered in any particular place?"

"No, but I think she'd like to be in your garden," Enid said. "Close to you, her dearest one."

"Enid, for God's *sake*," Ursula cried. He seemed not to have been aware of her presence until then. She wanted badly to go and put her arms around him and hold his head and kiss his hair. He looked so naked, stripped of himself.

Enid got up. "Now I must go and open the shop. There will probably be a quite profitable turnover today because people knew how close Nellie and I were."

Jeremy stood to face her. His voice was a little more alive, quiet, angry. "Why, over the telephone, were you so vicious to me, Enid? And why continuing up to this bitter end?"

"Just distraught, I'm afraid." The dramatic word came naturally to her tongue. "And then, Nellie called me Saturday night and said she wished you were home, that she'd been tempted to ask if she might stay at your house for the rest of the weekend. I don't know why. She's been a bit strange lately, worried. But I have this feeling that if you'd been here in New York, Nellie might be alive now."

Having delivered this unfair, unanswerable, and staggering blow, she made her exit.

Ursula said swiftly, "If I were you, I'd flush that. Right away."

"If, if, if," Jeremy said, thrusting his hands into his pockets. "If my father hadn't had a heart attack he wouldn't have died. If Nellie hadn't caught me sneaking out I would have gone skating on thin ice on the river and been drowned with the three other kids. If you miss your plane, and then it crashes on takeoff—"

"Stop." She put a hand on his shoulder, the touch light and delicate but summoning him back from a dark echoing place. The place of *if*.

Feeling like a man parachuted into another country and another time, Jeremy looked slowly and inquiringly around, trying to find some kind of balance.

The room he was in had color and character, obviously arranged to its tenant's sure and forthright taste and no one else's. Books, a lot of them, a blaze of mirror here and there among the watercolors and etchings and small oils—hers?—on the walls, green and white linen curtains to the dark shining floors, jewel-colored prayer rugs casually scattered. A great mass of white baby's breath on a wig stand in one corner, a large drawing board at one of the three windows, with a workmanlike littered red lacquer tabouret beside it.

Under other circumstances, a warm place to be, reliable and safe.

He walked over to the board and looked down at the drawing pinned to it, shadowy, merely hinted at: Nellie in a checked bibbed apron.

"She'd been going to pose for me on Sunday," Ursula said from across the room. "I wanted to get her colors right." Her colors. Pink of wool and hideous spreading blackening scarlet of blood. She put out a hand to grasp the mantelpiece.

He came over to her and took her in his arms and held her hard. She understood it, she thought, the terrible need for contact, for warm and living flesh. Without hesitation, she locked generous arms around his back. A reviving sweetness soaked her, a reward she hadn't looked for.

She heard herself saying crooningly, "I'm so sorry, so sorry, Jeremy . . . If you want to cry, cry. It's all right, you're among friends."

"Thank you but . . . can't stay lashed to your mast all day, I suppose." And then he started violently and dropped his arms, and looked down at George thrusting welcoming claws into one trouser knee. He bent and stroked the cat's head. "If you give me a little time I'll take him off your hands."

"No hurry, I'm fond of him." Either she had done him some fleeting good or he was getting himself back again; a sudden awakening electric energy from him went racketing around the room.

"And now I'll take myself off your hands. Can I leave that—frightful box here for the moment? Can I put it away in a closet for you? I've got nothing to carry it in."

Strange primitive revulsion, she didn't want to touch the box herself. She opened the door of the hall closet and he stretched his arm as far as it would go to the right, placing the ashes behind a yellow oilskin sou'wester on the shelf.

"Thank you, Jeremy."

"Thank *you*, Ursula. Will you be here if I—?" If he what? He wasn't entirely sure. Wanted her. Or needed her. At least as a bridge to Nellie, at least right now.

"I'm usually here, I work at home. Yes, I'll be here."

Jeremy went immediately to the Sixth Precinct station house and asked for and got a brief interview with the plainclothes detective in charge of the case, a man named Berenson.

Obviously busy as he was, Berenson was cooperative and amiable. He said he was sorry about Mr. Orr's aunt's death, and that she had seemed to be a well-liked lady. Everybody in her building was upset, and not just because they were afraid the same thing might happen to them, but because she was so nice, Nellie Hand.

Jeremy explained about having been away, out of the country, and asked if anything had surfaced, any pointer at all.

No, Mr. Orr, nothing had. But of course they'd keep on it. A ten-year-old child could have managed to get around Miss Hand's door lock. Too bad there hadn't been something of real and recognizable value and description taken, something to raise a red flag when it was pawned. "But there was only that necklace. Coral doesn't give you anything to go on. And the rings, nothing. And one Sony TV looks like all the rest, especially when the serial number's been filed off."

The autopsy. "Two fast jabs from behind. Luck, or skill, there's no way of telling. Not a long knife. But it got where it wanted to get."

Jeremy hesitated. Then he said, "You don't think there's any possibility it could have been set up to look like an everyday meaningless filthy—fumbled—job? Dust in the eyes, covering another reason?"

He knew the answer in advance but he had to say it.

Berenson gave him a patient smile and bore with him a minute or so. "Classic question: Who gains by her death? Well, you're the heir. She had something under two hundred in her checking account and savings of about fifteen hundred."

He looked briefly away from the other man's face.

"We're told, as I said, everybody liked Miss Hand. She wasn't dabbling in drug traffic or pornography or anything of that sort . . ."

Then he got to the basic point. "If we took up a position of looking on every casual bash—sorry—as the fiendishly clever work of a mastermind . . . Well, you see what I mean."

"I see exactly what you mean," Jeremy said. "Thanks for your time."

He took a cab to his house. There were no bookings for today or tomorrow as he hadn't been sure how long the Corning job would take. He packed a small suitcase with a change of clothes and dropped into the pocket along with toilet articles his palm-sized Minolta camera, as necessary to him as his toothbrush. He called Peggy on the studio extension, unable to face in person her kindness, her sympathy, and probably her tears on his behalf.

"If you need me before Thursday, Peg, I'll be at Yukon 9–2225."

Bursting to know details, Peggy gathered from the sound of his voice that this was the beginning and end of the conversation.

He found in the box that held his cuff links the front door and apartment keys Nellie had given him years ago. "It would be a comfort to know you had them, Jeremy."

He took another cab, downtown, to 20 Timothy Street.

Two

Occupation, however trivial, was a relief. Summoned by Susan Tingle, Ursula took a cab to Bonwit's, collected a box of garments, and went back downtown. She would press herself into service as a mirrored model.

It was an unfortunate year for clothing, in her opinion: bags of dresses bloused or lumped, immense awkward skirts striking dismally at mid-shin, often one doleful piece thrown over another, with no object as far as she could see except confusing the eye.

Hard to make the effect sexy, desirable. But she was a bold and much copied style-setter in her work and she thought she could manage again. She never used the careful wrist-manipulated pencil, but an immaculately pointed sable brush in a fast flexible thick-and-thin stroke. Her washes were swift and silky. Her Bonwit Teller girls looked like people, attractive and individual people; not drawing-board inventions.

A sitting position, she thought, for the first voluminous pile of amethyst Qiana. Pull it up to one knee, stretch a leg toward the mirror.

A bit difficult, though, with her pad on the floor beside her, having to look at herself, and then twist and bend over and register the remembered line with the brush. George, new to the field of fashion illustration, wanted to walk exploringly over the pad and she kept having to push him back. After completing one drawing she gave up and took Polaroids of herself in the other three dresses.

Before starting on the second drawing, she remembered that George had eaten up his one can of cat food and that she herself had had nothing today beyond a cup of black coffee back in some distant time, with Enid. She went to the delicatessen around the corner from the Evil Hour and bought milk, a loaf of her favorite Jewish rye bread, a wedge of cheddar, a head of romaine, two cucumbers, and George's food.

She was putting her key into the lock of 3A when she heard footsteps in the hall above. The 4A apartment, the only one on the floor besides Nellie's, was occupied by elderly Mr. Evers who lived, just barely, on his pension and Social Security. It had been Nellie's practice to invite him to dinner once a week and, she said, fill the poor man to the brim.

At the very faint sound her key made in the lock, the footsteps paused in what seemed an unaccountably sly way. Then he started down the stairs, and Ursula stood looking up at him, feeling a thud of recognition. *Why?* Not a face to remember. A tall boy, jawbone a little swung to one side, no color to his skin, hair, eyes, lashes.

"There was that boy who gave Nellie such a turn," Basil's voice said in her ear. "Bleached . . ."

Having recently studied her face in the mirror, objectively and thoroughly, Ursula felt on it the giveaway expression. Was that what had made him stop, long bony hand on the banister rail? She erased the look and turned the key. Hurry, get inside, call Basil, let him deal with the boy, if it was the boy.

She had almost closed the door behind her when it was kicked open again. She wheeled and he snatched her bag of groceries and hurled it to the floor.

"You looked as though you know me," he said. His voice was as glazed-over as his eyes. "But I don't know you."

She felt some kind of terrifying rage coming at her. As though it had been inside him, bottled up, and she was a near and convenient object to release it upon.

"Or maybe you just like my looks—"

She moved backward, one arm stretched out behind her. With a sudden stride, he put a hand inside her shirt collar and tore it open. Through her own screaming, she heard him panting, "You might as well really get to know me then—"

Her blindly seeking hand found the neck of the ginger jar lamp. His mouth was covering hers now, wet, clamping. With her one free arm, she swung the lamp hard against his thigh.

There was a sound from the doorway, somebody's voice, explosive. The boy in a lightning movement seized the lamp from her, turned, and flung it.

It caught Jeremy on his knee, and he stumbled and almost fell. Before he could recover himself the boy whipped past him and out the door and down the stairs.

Knee hampering him, Jeremy threw himself into pursuit. Seconds before he reached the little entrance hall, he heard the back door at the end of the dark corridor close. When he opened it again, the courtyard was empty except for a row of garbage cans exuding a sour-sweet odor in the sun. An alleyway led to the street, which when reached showed a number of people, but not a running, fugitive boy. Hopeless, with the house standing as it did right on the street corner.

He ran back to the courtyard and in at the rear entrance door, which in his haste he had left slightly open. Using the public telephone in the hall, he called the Sixth Precinct. One chance in a hundred a patrol car could spot the boy and pick him up, but still— "On the way to rape, as far as I could see." Even after the one stunned furious glimpse of the boy he described him with camera's-eye accuracy. Then he took the stairs two at a time.

Ursula's door was still ajar. She was sitting on a blue velvet hassock, head down, and over her stood a thin, stooped gray-haired man with a meat hammer in his hand.

She looked up when Jeremy came in. She was dull-eyed with shock and frighteningly pale. Jeremy removed the meat hammer from the man's hand and placed it on the coffee table.

"It was just that I—after poor Nellie—when I heard the screaming I was scared to death," Mr. Evers said. "Naturally I wanted to help but I didn't know what I might run into down here." In a city where people turned their backs on enactments of horror, a very brave man, Jeremy thought.

"But there was no one in the room but Miss Winter, and she . . . hasn't told me anything. Obviously she's had a fright."

"Mr. Evers got here a second or so after you left," Ursula said in a vague voice. "So you see it wouldn't have happened anyway. It wouldn't have happened in any case. And he might not have been able to go on with it no matter what, he was drugged up to here."

Obscurely embarrassed, Evers bent to pick up a cucumber near his foot.

"It's all right, I'll do that, and thank you very much," Jeremy said. Evers, with a final mildly curious look at them, picked up his meat hammer and left.

Remembering Enid's morning restorative, Jeremy went into the kitchen and saw the brandy bottle on the counter. George had tucked himself in an anxious huddle behind the kitchen door. He ran gratefully to Jeremy's ankle in an odd and unsettling world to which order had now been restored.

Jeremy sat on the floor beside the hassock. He handed her the glass. The mist, the vagueness, the withdrawal must be cut through.

"That's to drink, not just to stare at." His voice was crisp. "If this is your first near-rape in the city of New York at—what?— the age of twenty-eight, twenty-nine, you've led a charmed life. But statistically it's probably your last one too."

She drank half of her brandy. "There's nothing like looking on the bright side," she said, and from the whip-edged tone, and a grimace that tried to be a smile, he saw that his deliberate lack of sympathy, of concern, was working. "Twenty-eight."

"The police have an eye out for him right now. How did he get in here? Followed behind you and your groceries?"

"Yes. He came down from upstairs. If he didn't want Mr. Evers, he—" She looked at the floor trying to make herself think. "He must have been at Nellie's door for some reason. She'd bumped into him here before, and gave her a scare, and I think he saw that I recognized him."

He dug out all the information she could give him about the boy while he picked up her milk and cheese and bread and cat food.

She retrieved the second cucumber and sat studying it. With the other hand, she still clutched the now buttonless pongee shirt protectively to her.

"Two things. You can come upstairs with me and help go through Nellie's worldly possessions, which I'm sure you don't want to do, or you can get on with whatever you were up to." He had noted the large violet-patterned box spilling clothes, the

Polaroids on the coffee table, the dashing black-and-white drawing on her board.

"Yes, I must." For God's sake pull yourself together, stop being a burden, a wreck, a female with the vapors. *Nothing happened.* Nothing would have happened even without Jeremy, thanks to gallant Mr. Evers with his hammer.

All she had had was a nasty encounter. Jeremy had his hands full of death.

Squaring her shoulders, she stood up. "I have three more dresses to go. I'm due back uptown with everything no later than six."

"You must be a very fast gun at your work. Or brush, rather. If you're uneasy about anything, remember I'm right overhead."

It was, incredibly, after the forever morning, only noon. Using the key Berenson had given him, he opened the police-sealed door.

Someone had spread an orange towel over the place on the rug where Nellie must have lain. He lifted it and stood looking at the dark crusty blood. A fly dove greedily and he stamped on it.

Fighting a kind of darkness inside his head, he phoned in the classified ad to be run in the public notices columns of the New York *Times,* the *Villager,* and the *Village Voice.* It ought to make at least tomorrow morning's *Times.*

Suddenly aware that he had eaten nothing since a small portion of his tray breakfast on the plane at seven, he investigated Nellie's refrigerator. Eating without tasting it, an apple and then a piece of Gruyère, he made his mind work.

Tears running down Nellie's cheeks. "Just sort of three peculiar upsetting things in a row."

Her wanting to stay at his house for the rest of the weekend. Obviously for only one reason, because she was afraid of someone or something.

She had been quite right to be afraid. Whatever impossible thing she thought might be going to happen to her had happened.

He could see no threat whatever that Nellie could pose to anyone except as a possessor of possibly lethal secrets whispered into her sympathetic ear. Something confided, and afterwards regretted.

And then safely bound in permanent silence.

There was the boy, Ursula's would-be rapist, as terrifying and unpredictable as a stray dog with rabies. Because the random, the meaningless is the hardest of all to accept in the face of tragedy, he found himself inclined to dismiss the boy.

Except perhaps as some kind of pointer. Nellie, as willing to offer artless information about herself as to listen to others, might have told any number of people about him.

And given someone an idea.

A personal crime arranged to appear as a brutally casual, impersonal crime. A sad little daily-bread death.

He placed himself on the sofa where on Thursday night he had sat with her before the fire. He looked at the cold hearth and forced himself back in time. He had said that there was absolutely nothing she could not tell him.

It was troubling, and maybe unhealthy, morbid, trying to see her face beside him, hear her voice, the last time he would hear it before her death.

He saw her put the back of her hand to her forehead and heard her say it was first too cold and then too hot, and then she had said, on a long escaping breath, "Matthew."

Matthew . . . what? The telephone had rung, stopping her short, something about Charmian coming over the next day because the Lyleses' apartment was being painted. Something about Charmian being in love.

In Enid's account of all the people who loved his aunt—except him—present at her cremation, Matthew's name had not been mentioned. Was it because he was a man of large affairs, too busy to attend obscure obsequies? Or did he even know?

Instead of going to the telephone directory, he searched for Nellie's own address book and found it on her bedside table. It might prove to be useful in other ways too. A private who's who.

A bad time to call, but he tried anyway. The voice of an expensive executive secretary said Mr. Jones was out to lunch and had a conference immediately afterward. Jeremy told her his call was about a matter of great importance. "Can you just give me a key word or two to jot down?" she asked. "I have a pile of messages. I like to put first priority on top."

"The key word is Nellie," Jeremy said.

On the way to his two-thirty conference, Matthew stopped at Betty Mensham's immense white desk in a sea of zebra-patterned carpeting outside his office. "Just a few important ones." She handed him three slips of paper. The Nellie message intrigued her. The nice but authoritative-sounding man hadn't even given a last name. Nellie . . . a love affair?

Matthew was already striding away, reading his notes, when he came upon the third one.

He had by now turned a corner into a blind corridor and there was no one to see his face.

By the time he reached Conference Room No. 1, he looked jovially in command again. The two Matthews sat side by side, this time helpfully, one of them listening to other men and responding in a cool, measured way. How well his voice sounded in the long room, hung floor to ceiling in copper- and pink-striped Scalamandre silk velvet; how rich and deep, the timbre of his voice, how capable of quiet waiting to be heard. On top, you had no need to interrupt; silence, in fact, was a superbly useful tool.

The other Matthew walked in the rain, heading west, heading anywhere; it didn't matter. He had no idea whether he had walked one hour or two, occasionally turning north, then south, then east, trying to walk something away, or trying to decide whether it should be walked away or not.

He stopped in a smoky dismal homosexual bar where he was unlikely to encounter Village acquaintances and had two scotches, very fast, and then went out and walked again, soaked through and cold.

The transparent face had told him that it was over, he and Nellie. As friends, or whatever they were. As anything. Over.

He had shocked her away from him and she would never come back. He had lost the one person in the world he had thought might forgive him and by her forgiveness shrive him.

"Not even to celebrate the best thing that ever happened to me, Nellie?"

Not even then. Not ever.

Now she would owe him no loyalty, no self-silencing affection. And I trusted you with my life, Nellie.

He had another drink at a bar called Arturo's, not far from the East River, on Houston Street. Then he turned west again. It was late, close to midnight, but buildings were apt to bustle on Saturday nights, a lot of coming and going, not all of it in daylight sobriety.

He bought the Sunday *Times* at a newsstand on MacDougal Street and looked at himself as he might appear to the incurious Manhattan gaze: a man in a trench coat and hat, braving the rain to get his *Times* on Saturday night.

Rounding the corner into Timothy Street, he was met with a blast of music as an arriving couple went in at the door of the Evil Hour. He walked up the block and down again on the other side and saw a man with a large paper bag pressing a buzzer button at No. 20.

Moving swiftly, he caught the door just before it closed after the buzzed-in man; a clink from the hall suggested that he was delivering liquor.

Matthew slipped in and went down the corridor to the darkness under the stairwell, and waited. He heard the liquor delivery man coming down the stairs. The door closed behind him.

It opened again almost immediately; someone's key. "Well, then, okay, but just one drink," a girl's voice, thick, said. A high giggle. "My mother's visiting and she's fast asleep in my bedroom, remember that."

"Mother shmother," the man said. "Hurry up, I'm thirsty." Their footsteps indicated that her apartment was directly above.

Matthew waited another minute and then began his rapid climb. He met no one on the stairs. But he was rehearsing all the way up.

"I was in the neighborhood and I thought I'd drop in and say hello. But there was no answer when I knocked. I thought she was out somewhere . . . she's got more friends than the mayor."

He felt as if he were walking steadily toward his own death. Numb; with emotion, feeling, mercifully shut off.

He was startled, and puzzled, to see her door not quite closed. He had intended to knock until she answered, begging, praying her to let him in. "Just this one last time, Nellie. I must talk to you."

He gave the door a push with the flat of his hand and went in. Went in— And beyond that his mind refused to go.

He called Jeremy back at four. Registering astonishment, he thought, would be too exhausting, too much for him to handle.

Registering grief was no problem at all.

"Joy got through to me this morning," he said. "She told me. I feel as if one of my arms has fallen off." An authentic hoarse sound of tears in his throat.

"I thought you might be able to help. The police haven't anything to go on except the burglary setup."

"Christ, I'd do anything under the sun to help. But how?"

And, *why?*

Why is he asking me for help, by which he means information?

Jeremy had remembered, in the flood of trade gossip dispensed by Broom, the agency art director, on the way to Scotland, that it was pretty well decided Matthew Jones was on the brink of the presidency of UBC.

In his quiet voice he tossed a small blind grenade.

"I gather you were close to her, and might know what she was so worried about before she was killed. Or whom she was so worried about. Your name was the next to last one I heard from her. Before it happened."

After a silence, Matthew said, "You mean you think the scene was faked, and that someone she knew well killed her?"

"I'm not sure. But I don't think it's impossible."

"As soon as I'm able to use my head again," Matthew said, "I'll try to dredge up anything, anything at all, that might . . . But right now, Jeremy, I'm afraid I can't . . . talk . . . any more about it—"

"If something occurs to you," Jeremy said, "for the next few days I'll be right here. At Nellie's."

Three

A two-hour search of Nellie's apartment had produced nothing but more fuel for tight held-in grief. No letters breathing scandal, no diary with incendiary jottings. All was as open, as harmless, as Nellie herself.

He put aside three bills to be paid: Con Ed, New York Bell, and $27.50 to a Richard Grainger, D.D.S. All were recent; he gathered that Nellie kept up with her bills.

He wished desperately that he could retrieve the two days between the last time he had seen her, and her death: Friday and Saturday. Nellie was seldom solitary; there would have been people on her stage during those days, telephones ringing, feet on the stairway.

On impulse, he called Ursula. Did she know of any special trouble hanging over Nellie those last few days?

"Well, only that sister of Lise's, brutal to her . . . But all so silly, about money that probably doesn't exist."

"Tell me anyway."

She did, swiftly and succinctly. But probably nothing here, the sister not expecting the letter so imperiously demanded until Monday.

His last drawer-by-drawer hunt centered on the flowery white desk in the hall. He spent very little time at it after all, because it was jammed full of Charmian Lyle, her letters, her diaries, rafts of cards she'd saved—Valentine and birthday and Christmas cards going years back. He contented himself with going through the deep front drawer, and left it at that.

Nellie, he remembered, had signed her usual one-year lease in January. Her checkbook stub showed the April rent paid. The furniture, and her clothes, when he could bear to be practical, could be taken away, given away.

He thought how pleasant it would be to have Ursula's hand in his, a mutual reassuring grasp. Just for a few minutes. Comforting, necessary, the two of us— Oh, for God's sake. He tried to dismiss the hand, and the face, as an aberration of a dreadful Tuesday on Timothy Street.

On Nellie's dressing table was a photograph of him at the age of six, in a sailor suit, windblown tow hair in his eyes, sitting horseback fashion on a split-rail fence at the Orr house in Fairfield, Connecticut. "I have this feeling," Enid's voice said, "that if you'd been here in New York she would still be alive." He took the photograph out of the silver frame, tore it up, and threw it into the wastebasket; and was almost undone by seeing in the basket a neat square of paper tissue with a lightly blotted pair of pink lips on it.

Lukie held out until Tuesday afternoon.

She hadn't gone to Nellie's cremation service. Somebody had to cover the shop; and anything to do with death was disgusting anyway.

She was pretty sure she could kiss the money, her money, good-bye, but you never knew. The fact that Nellie had been killed indicated some kind of slipup, some disastrous haste, not a smooth clean job.

But if he hadn't found it, he might go back again.

It never occurred to her to question her conviction that Tost was responsible. He had, she was sure, been the one who took her own apartment to pieces. She had flown to Nellie's, and two days later Nellie was next in line. She had no idea from whom he had known, or heard, that she had taken temporary cover at 20 Timothy Street, but Tost had a wide circle of acquaintances overlapping her own.

Having extracted a handful of notes from the envelope before she tucked it away, she took a room at the battered but bustling Hotel Marlton on Eighth Street a few doors down from Fifth Avenue.

For her Titian wig she substituted a long curly black one, and gave herself a slight limp. In a way it was frightening, this hour-to-hour job of being anybody but Lukie; in a way it was crazy fun. It was comforting that any time she chose to, she could cut

and run to Dean in Atlantic City. But if I don't make *sure* about
the money, she thought, I'll have this itch forever. The only way
to handle an itch was to scratch it.

She called Nellie's number three times, the first call at ten in
the morning. Weird to hear the phone ringing in a dead woman's
apartment. But sooner or later wouldn't someone be there? Some
relative, some friend, to see to the disposal of Nellie's things, to
clean out the refrigerator and turn it off, and ghastly things like
that? Turning Nellie off. She remembered a throng of people
hurrying about being useful the day after her mother's funeral.

Her third call was at two o'clock. A man's voice, raw-sounding.
Lukie identified herself—it was the kind of voice that had nothing to do with Tost's world—and asked if she could come around
for a few minutes. Yes, she could.

As she approached the house on the corner, she felt an unac-
customed shrinking into herself, as though expecting some blow
from behind. What if he was hanging around somewhere near,
waiting for a chance to slip in? What if he X-rayed right through
her wig, her limp, her dark glasses, her black-caped Regency
cotton cloak?

She saw a familiar face across the street. Redheaded Nix,
Nicholas Freyerhauser the Fourth, sitting on a large trash can
taking the air between his chores at the Evil Hour. As children,
they had smeared each other's hair with raspberry jam at the
legendary Little Red Schoolhouse.

"Hey, Nix!"

He put out his cigarette and came indolently across the street.

"Will you walk me up the stairs to Nellie's apartment? I could
use an escort."

"I *guess* you're Lukie, true and blue behind all that stuff and
underneath it," Nix said. "She's dead."

"I know. Isn't it awful?"

"Well, what's your problem? Afraid of ghosts or something?"

"If Tost comes around asking questions, you never saw me
here, or anywhere for that matter."

"Unless I'm paid for it, I never utter." He took her arm and
upon delivering her to the fourth-floor landing left her with an
absentminded light kiss. She knocked and Jeremy Orr opened
the door to her.

He had changed into his working clothes, fresh chinos and a dark blue jersey. Before he opened his mouth, some essence of him came to Lukie and hit her hard. Something quite new to her: a male authority and grace.

She was charmed and touched by the stuck-together dark lashes and one small suspicious drop of water beside his attractive mouth. In an apologetic way not usual with her, she said, "I'm so sorry to come bursting in at a time like this, but I stayed with Nellie Thursday night and left a couple of things behind. You're Jeremy, aren't you? She's told me about you."

She saw the towel on the floor and looked quickly away from it. That must have been the place where—

"And what was it you left behind?" He was looking at her in what she thought was an odd and totally examining way.

"I'd cashed my pay check and I didn't want to carry the money around with me until I—" Invention failed her. Her eyes went to the desk in the hall.

"Do you get paid twenty-nine thousand and fifty-eight dollars a week?" he asked. "Or is it every two weeks?"

Years dropped away and a suddenly fierce child cried, "It's *mine!* Give it to me!"

"Under the circumstances—there's apparently been a robbery here as well as a death—I think you'd better explain your wad." The quietness in his voice holding her back there, at the age of nine or ten.

Lukie blushed, another sensation new to her. "I'm keeping it for a friend."

"I think it might be wise to let the police keep it for your friend. They might be interested in the fact that it was left behind. And not all that hard to find, for anyone going through drawers."

"Oh please, not the police, you could get me into . . . terrible terrible trouble . . ." Fear widened her eyes and turned down her mouth corners.

"Well, I'll hold it for the time being."

He continued to study her narrowly. The wig and the extravagantly witchlike garments, the deathly lavender-white makeup gave him not a moment's pause. In his professional world, looking different at all costs was a kind of norm. The most expensive model in New York had taken to arriving for sittings at his studio in impeccable black English sidesaddle riding dress.

His survey made her nervous, the more so because she was almost hypnotically drawn to him. "I suppose you'll give me a *receipt* for the money, and then I'll—" She gathered her cloak around her in a motion of departure.

His hand fastened around her wrist. "Sit down and tell me about your friend. You seem to be badly frightened of him."

Astonished, she found herself sitting, and found herself talking, while he stood over her.

"His name is Tost, Arnold Tost. He's Dutch, I think. He was in prison for"—grave legal recital—"assault with intent to cause grievous bodily harm. A truckload of furs, and he had a gun on him. A state police car just happened to be going by. He got two years. Then he got out, and since then he's been looking for me and his money, which as far as I'm concerned is mine. Not that the money matters, not all that much. But the awful thing is that Nellie . . ." She stopped to stare, and sighed. ". . . had to get killed because of it."

"Would you mind filling in a few final blanks?" How could a voice so quiet cut so deep?

"He found out from someone where I lived and tore up my apartment. I asked Nellie if I could stay with her that night. I was scared. I put the envelope where you found it. I know now it was a terrible thing to do but when I knew it was time for him to get out I told practically everybody I'd be staying with Nellie. He came looking for me here before Thursday and frightened her. In his head, Nellie and I and this apartment and the money were, you know, all one thing, sort of. I don't know why he waited till Saturday but maybe he was frying some other fish of his. I guess after he killed her he didn't dare stay and look some more."

In a doleful, memorial voice, she added, "In ways it's all my fault. I can't bear it . . ." And protestingly, close to tears, "But Nellie was so *nice*."

As simple as that, said a dull voice in Jeremy's head. As simple, casual, meaningless as that. A boy named Tost bent on retrieving twenty-nine thousand dollars. Doughty Nellie resisting, defying him.

An ordinary colorless death at the hands of an ordinary colorless criminal.

He had called Berenson and five minutes later a reluctant Lukie was picked up by a patrol car and taken to the Sixth Precinct to make a formal statement.

At the door, she turned to Jeremy and said flatly, "Now look what you've done. People may see me in the police car, or coming out of the building with them, looking as though I'm under arrest. If he finds out he'll kill *me*."

He accepted a responsibility that was in no sense his. "When you're finished at the station you can stay at my house. There are usually people there, in the studio, and I'll see to it that there's someone around the clock, for a while."

Peggy Earl, when called, said she would take care of the matter of keeping a close eye on Lukie Callender. And yes, her brother Jim, who was the darkroom assistant (six feet three and formidable) would be glad to stay at the house for a week or so; it would be a nice change for him. "Anywhere he lives on his own is instant flophouse."

At five o'clock, Jeremy found that he had been working steadily at Nellie's once three-quarters-full bottle of scotch. Oh well, everybody gets drunk at wakes. Only this is a post-wake, no coffined body to pay one's respects to and if inclined say one's prayers over. Nothing but a turquoise-enameled box on Ursula Winter's closet shelf.

What was he doing here at this hour, anyway?

It was all wrapped up, however sloppily.

Assault with intent to cause grievous bodily harm. The intent successfully carried out.

Oh yes, her clothes and furniture to be seen to. But not now, not today, garments to be touched, whiffs of Nellie to greet and scald the nose, the perfume she loved. Caron's Nuit de Noël, a bottle of which he gave her every Christmas along with a stocking full of other little packages.

But why, here on this sofa, in front of this fireplace, her sadness? Her withholding of something she seemed to want to tell him but for some reason couldn't bring herself to.

Tost wouldn't have made anyone sad; after her first fright Tost would have made Nellie mad. "There's this sinister boy hanging around in the hall, I don't like the looks of him. Do you think I should call the police? They're among other things what we pay taxes for, after all."

A *hired executioner.* But she'd used that phrase to point out to him how silly she was being, how far her worries about three peculiar things had carried her.

In any case, the idea was grotesque, as impossible to accept as the one he probably must swallow and live with: a sneak thief with a knife.

Finish this drink. And do what?

His tilted world took a further turn. Fancies appeared in Nellie's living room. Sharp and vivid, mentally photographed.

Click! went the shutter. Gretel, or Gretel's husband, removing Lise's heir to a fortune perhaps not mythical. Ursula's word-for-word recital of Nellie's account of the Gretel woman's visit: "You can't mean to tell me you intend to suck the blood of a dying woman . . . It's not only me, it's my children . . ." The dreadful single-minded force of a certain kind of motherliness.

Click! Matthew on her mind, that very last time, here before this fireplace, his name spoken and then the telephone interruption. Some serious peccadillo murmured into Nellie's ear before he reached the top of his cliff in full exposing sunlight, the brand new president of a major network. *Oh God,* Matthew thinking, *Nellie might spill it out at any time, not knowing that now it would be a disaster.*

Or Joy, that handsome and fearfully efficient wife of Matthew's. "Darling, I'll go see her and get it all straightened out." In this shot, she wore a tailored suit and a haggard face.

The shutter clicked again. Walter Lyle, finding that Charmian had met her lover at Nellie's, with Nellie's consent and approval, telling her with his knife what he thought of this arrangement. Then taking a handkerchief to a spurt of blood on his immaculate dark gray suit.

Enid now appeared in the camera's eye. A friend of twenty years' standing. There must be absolutely nothing Nellie hadn't known about Enid. A quarreling, a falling-out, a possible loss of Nellie's job, and then a threat of retaliation on Nellie's part?

No. This shot didn't work; it came out blurred and ghostly. But Enid's uncharacteristic bitter hostility while informing him of the details of Nellie's death? "I am distraught," said the expensively educated voice.

Don't go on with it. An unhealthy harvest reaped from scotch, ashes, and physical exhaustion, he assured himself. He picked up the bottle, noted the level to which it had sunk, and put it down again.

The brisk knocking at the door was like an allegorical summons back to reality.

The man to whom he opened the door had a raging sunburn, concentrated at fever pitch on his large nose. Out of breath, he said, "I'm Morrison, Three B—just back from Fire Island, a long weekend—bathroom ankle-deep in water—I thought it might have started up here at the top, at Nellie's. Of course now that I think of it she wouldn't be home yet—"

Wearily leaping an immense ditch, Jeremy said, "No, she isn't. I'll go look." The bathroom was dry and shipshape.

"I'll call the plumber from here right now if you don't mind. At this rate the floor might fall and the landlord's usually ankle-deep in gin. You learn to fend for yourself at Twenty Timothy Street."

His call made, he put a distracted heel of his palm to a flaming forehead. "Oh lord, Basil's gallery, I wonder if he knows the floodgates are open. Shall we go and warn him?"

Glad of the presence of the roseate stranger and the relief of mundane household crises, Jeremy went with him down the stairs.

The hall door into the Ditto Gallery was ajar, and it was immediately evident that the open floodgates had proclaimed themselves to Basil. Paintings were stacked every which way near the door leading to the basement storeroom and Basil's subterranean voice could be heard raised in furious nonstop swearing.

"We're here to help!" shouted the neighborly Morrison. "Plumber's on the way!" To Jeremy, he said, "You wouldn't mind lending a hand, Mr.—?"

"Orr. Not at all."

The water on the floor of the dimly lit basement room was at least two inches deep. Basil thrust an armload on Morrison and Jeremy began snatching up paintings in the corner nearest him. There must be fifty or more in the room, leaning on edge against the cement block walls.

"For Christ's sake, hurry!" Basil roared. "*Look at the ceiling!*" The plaster was bulging and dripping where the pipe entered to the left of the stairway.

Jeremy placed his pile halfway up the steps and headed for the corner under the pipe. He cleared it rapidly and, resting his chin on top, carried his burden up to the gallery. Basil, plunging past him for another trip down the stairs, crashed into the pile and knocked it sideways.

A canvas revealed itself about halfway down the jostled pile. Jeremy stood staring at it. A pulled-back blue curtain behind a rush-seated chair, a distance of light-drenched apple orchards in bloom, and a spiraling poplar under curling clouds. Its beauty and authority rang through the room.

He bent and touched the impasto surface of a cloud and a tingle of recognition shocked his fingertip.

The picture looked to be thirty-six by forty-eight inches. Its frame was the showy, heavily worked gilded wood used for all Basil's larger productions. A nice throwaway touch. He tried to remember from which European museum or private collection it had been stolen several months ago.

He took his Minolta out of his back pocket—luckily the close-up lens was on, unluckily the light was poor—and pressed the button. Hearing Morrison panting his way up the stairs, he covered the Van Gogh with a well-executed copy of Gauguin's "The White Horse" and rejoined the work team.

In ten minutes more, the three men had the basement cleared. Through the big plate-glass window, street onlookers gazed with idle curiosity at the scene of confusion within. Basil, sweating, his color all gone, his face taut and greenish, was swabbing at the edges of frames. A hand rattled the doorknob; Basil shouted, "Can't you read? *Closed.*"

He collapsed abruptly into a canvas sling chair.

"You all right, old man?" Morrison asked.

"Bottle in the refrigerator. And get some glasses too."

Jeremy took one sip of his icy straight vodka and put his glass on a shelf of art books. Get him now, while he was winded and down, the confident Basil.

"I noticed a nice Van Gogh copy—'The Blue Curtain.' What's the price? I might take it off your hands."

A heavy dense silence fell. There was a shimmer and shaking of danger in the air like not-very-distant lightning.

Morrison said, "Drink your drink down, Basil, do you good. You look beat."

"Not for sale." Hard breathless syllables, fired rather than spoken at his would-be customer. His gaze locked with Jeremy's.

"Or rather," Basil amended through thinned lips, "it's bought and paid for. I'm holding it until it's wanted."

Holding it indeed. A question stabbed at him. Had Nellie known about this potentially deadly secret deep under the operations of the Ditto Gallery?

What better place to receive, handle, and dispose of stolen paintings? No wonder, Basil, you can wear a mink-lined coat when the weather turns nippy.

Careful. The lightning was nearer. Get out from under the tree.

"Oh, too bad. Then what about the Cézanne 'Harlequin'?"

Basil took his time answering. His examining eyes roved Jeremy's face. Then, "Three hundred and fifty. But you only saw —what?—several dozens or so of my masterpieces. Wouldn't you like to go through them at your leisure? Although you don't look the type or the income for copies, however expert they may be."

One question, loaded. One challenge, also a question, also loaded. Jeremy let them both go by with the carelessness of innocence.

"Nellie gave me a print of the Cézanne when I moved into my first little nowhere apartment. It's a kind of reminder of her."

"You shall have my 'Harlequin,' as a reminder of Nellie, for nothing," Basil said, princely. His voice had recaptured its richness and his color was coming back. "My last tribute to, and for, Nellie, God rest her soul."

Remain facing Basil, don't invite him to interpret the nature of the small oblong object in your back pocket, noticeably thicker than a wallet. The strenuous exercise just completed provided a better solution. Jeremy yanked his damp jersey out of his pants and let it flop loose, emitting an overheated grunt as he did so.

He supposed as a law-abiding citizen he should pass his discovery—and his suspicion that it was only one of such prizes passing silently through the Ditto Gallery—along to the police. But not now, not until he decided whether or not it could be of personal use to him.

Basil rose from his sling chair. "I thank both you gentlemen for your kind services. No offense, Morrison, but to have an eminent photographer fetching and carrying and sweating for one is indeed an honor."

Jeremy read the narrowed eyes still on him. He's not sure, but he thinks I know, and he wonders what's under my jersey and if I've collected any visible proof.

Photographers as a race seldom venture forth without some kind of camera or other. You never knew at what unexpected moment you might get, or miss and mourn forever, the shot of a lifetime.

What would he do if he were Basil? If one word could rip apart the texture of his life, certainly of his living? Short of making sure by physical methods that the word could never be spoken, he would remove any and all evidence as soon as no one could catch him at it. The small color slide in the Minolta, no matter how enlarged, would not be conclusive; the canvas itself would be needed for sophisticated X-ray tests.

And then later, if Jeremy did choose to air the matter, Basil's comments, now that he had got his balance back: "Van Gogh? What a compliment to Basil van Gogh Perov!" (Gust of laughter.) "Of course, the poor chap had just stumbled onto his aunt's demise and—wouldn't you in his place?—had been resorting heavily to funeral-baked scotch."

Yes, much safer, right at the moment, to leave Basil alone with his treasures.

He accepted the Cézanne with thanks, and left Morrison debating with himself in the hall whether Noxzema was the best bet for his sunburn or whether he should boil some strong tea and apply it. "They say tannic acid . . ."

From Nellie's window overlooking the courtyard, he watched for a few moments, standing well back. A dark red Volkswagen pulled into the courtyard. Basil got out of it, went through the back door, and came out in five minutes carrying a large flat wrapped package. He placed the package on the floor behind the front seat and nosed the car down the alley, which was just wide enough to allow its passage.

There, said Jeremy, goes Van Gogh.

Four

Lise sat in the near-darkness of her apartment wondering if she should allow herself another drink of Jack Daniels.

But after all, if there was ever a time to celebrate—

And, if there was ever a time to be sad—

She felt like an exhausted runner too tired and numb and far gone to exult at the tape breaking across her chest. Charles Lambert, her lawyer, had called her an hour ago.

"Yes, all over, you've won hands down, no concessions, no compromises."

"If you can call seven years in court hands down," Lise said. And then, still a little unable to believe in it but with the first stirrings of greed, "When does it begin, the money?"

"Several weeks at the outside. I won't bother you with the details, but anything you want can be advanced immediately through the Bank of New York."

"I'll let you know tomorrow. I must take this in all the way from head to toe." Then, sharply, "I assume you have informed me before notifying my sister? Considering the difference in our equities in the estate?"

Oh yes, indeed, Lambert had gone to the top first and foremost. No slightest misstep must be made at this point, when he was looking forward to what in the course of his career would be a landmark fee.

But, Lise thought, how cruel, how bitter the timing. Almost too late for her, unless the doctors were wrong. Although she had long since made the discovery that while cheery prognoses might turn out to be overly optimistic, dire ones were usually correct. Two years, three? Or any week—who knows?

And entirely too late for Nellie. Why, she could have had, tomorrow, her set of Sèvres, her furs, her diamond earrings. And her stay at the Bristol on Rue du Faubourg Saint Honoré, all but across the street from the President's palace, for—who cared?— perhaps two hundred a day . . .

And then later, true and lasting repayment for all her kindness over the years, her company, her soup, her library books, her patient listening to tales of symptoms, of pain. Her invariable buoying up, leaving behind her always a certain cheerfulness and calm.

Thinking about this, Lise's heart began to behave in an alarming fashion, thudding heavily. What if I haven't two or three years? Must get Lambert here tomorrow— At the thought of Gretel inheriting by default, the thudding intensified. Next of kin. That beast?

But not the home for cats this time. That had just been to amuse herself; Gretel had had a pathological fear of cats from earliest childhood. Back, then, to her next dearest in the world after Nellie. Enid.

At eight o'clock, Jeremy went down one flight of stairs, his purpose, he thought, being to collect Nellie's ashes, and George. And if Ursula had recovered herself, to ask her to dinner. He was suddenly and fiercely lonely, and he was hungry.

At his knock, a man's voice inside said, "Stay there, I'll get it." The door was opened a little impatiently. "Yes?"

A pleasant-looking craggy man probably in his late thirties. He gave an impression of being interrupted at something interesting.

From beyond, Ursula called, "Come in, Jeremy. Jeremy Orr, Sam Gamble."

She had come home, tired and still shaken, feeling otherworldly. She had shed her clothes, showered, splashed herself with Spanish lavender, and put on a long, loose drift of white dotted swiss. With a book, with quiet, things might pull themselves together into some kind of shape to be lived with.

Sam Gamble had called before she could even open her book. "Just one drink, please? I know you're upset, that poor Hand woman, but I do want to see you."

She decided instantly not to tell him about her drugged and dangerously amorous visitor. There would be rage, and too much sympathy, and arms wanting to comfort her, while her comfort —not yet conquered and firmly put away—lay in only one, unavailable place.

Now here he was. Tired but forceful, agile and dark, and in some way concentrated on and around her. From across the room she almost felt the skin of her wrist touched.

Jeremy looked at her in the sofa corner and noted the down pillow beside her, squashed.

His hand went itchily to his back pocket, and then he thought it wouldn't do just now. But he would have liked to have had the picture. Swathe of hair on one side of her face taking in and giving off a shining copper light. The white dotted swiss pale green here, lilac there, remote blue in its folds, blue as the shadows on her temples. Elegant high-arched bare feet, the one sole that he could see flushed with rose.

He said, "I've come for that cat and a few . . . other things."

Gamble, not liking the domestic, sharing sound of this, offered, "The cat's in the kitchen. They make me sneeze, so Ursula bottled him up there." He sounded deferred-to, at home, and possessive.

Jeremy seemed not to get the message. At his ease, he strolled over to the window, studied the evening, and turned around. Gamble was still in a hopeful stance not far from the door, waiting to let him out, with his cat.

The silence stretched. Ursula said, "Will you have a drink, Jeremy?"

"If you're sure I'm not in the way—" His dark eyes met Gamble's frown serenely.

Looking back at Ursula, he did get her message, he wasn't quite sure how. Don't mention Tost, not now.

"Sit still, I'll help myself now that I know my way around your kitchen."

Ursula felt the corners of her mouth wanting to lift a little but kept her face expressionlessly polite. "But do close the door. Because of Sam."

Then guilt touched her. Some kind of secret game, which she herself didn't understand thoroughly, was being played on Sam. Nice Sam, who said he loved her, who said and showed he wanted her. A game played with this aloof stranger who, like a

man at a cocktail party, had picked her up off the plate, a fine
crisp cold shrimp on a toothpick, gazed at the shrimp, decided
he hadn't the appetite for it, and put it back on the plate again.

And then had brought his actress, Anya something, the two
of them obviously physically involved with each other, to say
succinctly to anxious matchmaking Nellie, *Lay off, Nellie dear.*

It was one thing to embrace a man in his grief; another to assume that this was the opening of a firmly closed door.

When he could be hoped to be out of hearing in the kitchen,
Sam said furiously, "What the hell kind of oaf—has he no manners?" He came and sat down beside her and took her hand and
kept it. "Who in Christ's name is he anyway? Besides someone
named Orr."

Sam was a designer of electronics and owned his own small
and extremely successful firm; he did not keep up with professional names unencountered in the *Wall Street Journal.*

"He's Nellie's nephew. And, of course, the photographer."

"The photographer! Excuse my ignorance!" Not a man accustomed to using the idiom with ease, point, and dexterity, he
nevertheless added, "Shots of this. Shots of that. Go shoot your-
self, Orr."

"Sssshhh . . ."

Jeremy said hello to George and mixed himself a drink that
was mostly water. A nice, long-lasting depth of liquid. He came
back into the living room and settled himself comfortably in
the smoky blue velvet wing chair.

Looking, goddammit, in that chair, like the man of the house,
Sam thought, knuckles whitening as he gripped his glass.

Ursula wanted her hand back but felt that to remove it was
another sort of betrayal. Jeremy looked at the ownerly clasp in
an interested but impersonal way.

"I noticed you have a couple of cans of cat food, may I take
them along? In due time, that is." He tasted his drink, closed his
eyes peacefully, a man relishing this island of repose, and then
opened them again, and smiled at Ursula.

This would not do, not at all. Ursula sensed the barely held-
back rising storm inside Sam, which at any minute could break;
he had an open and uneven temper. Jeremy might choose to
tease him, manipulate him, but she would not join in.

She invented a quick social lie. "I am sorry, but we do have a dinner reservation and I'd better . . ."

She got up, a woman decisively on her way to dress.

Strange, to have to protect and encourage a man she didn't want, dismiss a man she did want. All because under the circumstances it was the only decent and possible thing to do.

And, the only narrow alley along which at this particular moment she could find her way.

Jeremy this time took his cue. After collecting George, he stopped at the living-room door and said, "Remember I'll be right upstairs during the night if you need me."

Sam made a grunting disapproving noise, which might have been what caused Jeremy to add, "Another thing to bear in mind, Ursula—Nellie more or less left you to me."

He carried up the stairs with him the vivid memory of her look of astonished anger somehow seasoned with amusement, her mouth trying to frame an answer to this outrageous statement. But he had been too quick for her.

Sam had resumed scowling. "What did he mean, left you to him?"

She didn't want to analyze it. Was he being bitter-funny, or was he gently and understandably drunk? Was it mere concern for a friend of his aunt's who had had a bad, frightening encounter because of her? Or what?

Continuing out loud, she said, "Oh well, Sam, Nellie was fond of both of us, and as to what he said, how would you feel if you came back from abroad and found someone very important to you had been—was dead and gone?"

"In that light, yes, horrible. Shocking. Would certainly put you off your stride. Can't blame him if he makes no sense. No sense at all."

"All well at this end," Peggy Earl reported by phone. She was used to dealing with Lukies, young women insolently or innocently in love with themselves, depending on your point of view. "She wanted your bedroom. Liked the water bed. I said you might be occupying. So much the better, she said. You're wanted for some still shots, color, McCann Erickson. A perfume, Artistry.

Free hand—whatever you like after you shoot to the layout. Shall
I book for tomorrow?"

"Thursday," Jeremy said.

"I'll put Jim on the living-room sofa for tonight, okay? He
might as well guard-dog the whole house. Two beers I told him,
no more, you're to sleep very lightly. And preferably uneasily.
One more thing. Lukie says you've been so nice to her that someone named Nix might help you, about someone named Tost.
Works across the street from where you are. The Evil Hour. Only
she says don't tell the police or he'll clam up. Have you eaten?"

"No, not yet."

"Bluebonnet, terrible name. But not prim inside. Eleventh
Street. The best veal piccante I ever tasted."

He called the Sixth Precinct, knowing that by now Berenson
would probably be off duty. "Whoever's on the Hand case,
please," identifying himself as a relative of the deceased. "Timothy Street, robbery and murder, Saturday night." In a far corner
of his brain a voice still asked, Is it really as simple, as dreadfully
simple, as all that?

A man named Calder said, "No, nothing on Tost yet. Got the
usual machinery working."

They both knew that by now the notably no-color Tost might
well have a head of brown hair, or black; and could be in
Newark, or just around the corner from the Sixth Precinct, or on
the planet Venus, for all the hope they ever had of finding him.

His fingerprints were on record but matched none of the
prints taken by the police at the apartment. Gloved, probably.
"Yeah, well, that's it for the moment, Mr. Orr."

"When will the police seal be off the door?"

"Should've been off by now. It'll be seen to tomorrow, early."

At this point it would be a help to have the freedom of Nellie's
apartment accessible to anyone who might decide that he or
she had a pressing errand there.

Nix and the Evil Hour first, something to eat second.

As he opened the door, there was a sense of motion immediately outside it, a backing up.

He looked at Walter Lyle, now standing two feet away from him.

"I just," began Walter Lyle. "I just—mmm—"

Everything about him was as well turned out as always, except his face, which seemed to have lost its precise perfection of feature and was in some way out of shape, a suggestion of sag. His eyes were too lightlessly dark to show shock but Jeremy felt it coming from him.

How long had he been standing there outside the door and—no knock—what had he been listening for?

Walter looked down at his attaché case and seemed to draw some reassurance from this article of daily business equipment. "I was to meet Jove here. Nellie has Charmian's desk." He made it sound like an illegal appropriation of property.

Jeremy raised his eyebrows. "Were you going to help him carry it down?"

"No, but I had no idea as to whether in their search the police might go through my wife's private papers. I had intended to remove them. Immediately. I didn't know there was anyone here or I would have made myself known. Jove said he could get a key from someone but I suppose he hadn't bargained for this." He gestured at the police lock.

Regretting it afterward, but tired, and obsessively fishing in a buried river, Jeremy said, "I'm afraid the money, the close to thirty thousand dollars in it, is gone. The police have it."

It was as if he had struck Walter Lyle across the face with the flat of his hand. He took a fumbling step backward.

From the depths of the stairwell came a din of skirling music, growing steadily louder. "Lead kindly light," bawled the bagpipe.

The piper paused for breath, making his way up the final flight. Jeremy recognized him as part of the Village landscape, a huge kilted Scot who strode the streets playing his pipes, showered from windows, when the mood took the tenants, with coins which he caught in his bonnet.

"A last serenade for bonnie Nellie!" he panted. "Let it be known, let it be heard, that she is mourned by those who love her!"

He put his lips to the mouthpiece and poured his breath into "My Darling Nellie Gray."

Jeremy caught only part of what Walter said above the explosion of music, as he turned to go down the stairs. ". . . get away from this nightmare . . ." He was gone, running.

Jeremy politely let the Scotsman, known as Highland Harry, finish his selection. The door of 4A opened cautiously and Mr. Evers put his head out to look and listen.

"Very kind of you," Jeremy said, after the last piercing note. He gave Highland Harry a ten-dollar bill. "Go and have a drink to her." The piper was known to be devoted to his country's national beverage.

The bonnet was doffed and he played himself down the stairs to "Will Ye No Come Back."

Later, Jeremy wasn't entirely sure whether it was his random mention of the money or the opening bars of the serenade which had hit Walter like a hammer blow. Surely, clearly, its keeper if not its owner had been established? But maybe Walter thought Charmian had been holding it ready there, among her diaries and her memories, in case of some sudden pressing emergency.

Nellie: *"I'm afraid she's fallen in love."*

The Evil Hour occupied a large high-ceilinged room a long flight down from Timothy Street. Its decor was principally flashing dizzying light, moony blue, silver, and white. The glistening dance floor was lacquered black. In the center of the floor was an immense drum, six feet high and five feet in diameter. There were black banquettes on three walls, with round-topped black plastic tables spaced closely in front of them. There was no live music; a man in a scarlet-lit booth at the rear, scarlet himself in the light, manipulated his records and tapes and on and off sang to them. He made up words when he forgot how they went, his improvisations obscene, amusing, or both, according to his mood. Occasionally, in the middle of a steaming sequence, he would roar *"Censored!"* to laughter and clapping.

The room was only about a quarter filled when Jeremy went down the stairs at nine thirty. He slid into a banquette corner and was immediately attended to by a girl wearing black stretch lace panty hose and nothing else.

"Drink, sir? Or food? Or both?" She handed him a large black menu printed in white. "Plenty of time before the hour."

"What hour?"

"The evil one. When they put out the lights and yell, 'Okay, let's be evil, everybody!' Honestly, you have no *idea*—!"

She seemed like a nice, open-faced girl. Jeremy asked, "Is there anything here that's all right to eat?"

"If it was me, I'd take the beefburger. It's expensive, but it's prime, they get it from Tory's on Ninth Street, and it's kind of simmered in wine and they put sautéed mushrooms on the roll instead of ketchup and relish and all that junk."

"Then yes, and a bottle of Heineken's, and I'd like to talk to Nix right away if he's around."

The twenty-year-old who came to the table five minutes later might have been guest instead of help at the Evil Hour: fashionably untidy red hair, patrician features, jeans, madras shirt.

"Shades of the days of the speakeasy," Jeremy said. "Lukie sent me. Sit down and have a drink."

He had to raise his voice; a crouching young black man had begun circling the great drum, beating it into slumbering thunder. The girl he had lifted to its top began a scarf dance, the scarves black and loosely floating and flying about her lithe bare white body which was painted all over with sprigs of pink roses. The dancers on the floor seemed to be paying little or no attention to her.

Jeremy had decided to widen his focus. A pair of alert blue eyes right across the street . . . He told Nix who he was and why he was here. "I'm curious about my aunt's Saturday. I wondered if you noticed anyone—anything out of the ordinary. Sorry to sound so undirected."

Nix took a swallow of his Chablis. In a friendly fashion, he said, "You look and sound as undirected as a coral snake heading for somebody's ankle." Another thoughtful swallow. "I told Lukie though that I did nothing for nothing."

"I'm not asking for anything for nothing."

In Jeremy's brief thorough assessment, Nix was not a devoted peddler of possibly false information. He plainly and simply could use some money. Writer, poet, artist? Getting along on a thin edge in the Village, where some people believed there was still inspiration in the very air?

Nix grinned. "All right, so I don't look like a potboy. I'm writing a play. Title: *On Timothy Street*. No plot, just the people and the comings and goings. Oh, and I'm a month behind in my rent. A hundred and five dollars."

"Okay, rent paid if you can be of any kind of help."

"I don't know if I can or not. Saturday nights I spend what time I can get off sitting on my favorite trash can up there, collecting stuff. One of my pearls was, a woman went by with another woman and I caught 'She thought she had trichinosis but it turned out she was pregnant'—"

At the impatient thump of Jeremy's glass on the table, he applied himself to the subject. "Your aunt came out around nine thirty with her string shopping bag. I warn you this may be zero stuff but you asked. On her way back in, a little while later, a man waiting in a car near the door got out and they talked a little and then he took her arm and they went in together. I had an idea that she didn't want him to come in with her but she didn't call for help or anything."

"What did he look like?"

"Like someone from my father's law firm. Freylinghauser and Wickersham. Same type, I mean. Businessman to his bones, even a hat, a homburg yet. Fifties, I'd say, gray hair, pince-nez—I didn't know anyone wore them any more. The car had New Jersey plates. A Volvo, black."

He looked at his empty wineglass. A swiveling spotlight turned him milk-blue. Jeremy signaled the girl in the lace panty hose and held up two fingers.

"I have no idea how long he stayed. I had to go back in. I didn't get out again until after the evil hour."

"And what"—academic curiosity, almost—"are your duties during it?"

"Evvie—our wine and beer bearer—screams and I run after her in the dark and we collapse on a banquette and try to make everybody feel at home doing whatever they're up to."

"You didn't see the car later, the Volvo?"

"If I did I don't remember. Sorry. Certainly not much material for a month's rent . . ."

"Have you any idea where somebody named Arnold Tost lays his head?"

"No, not since he's out. Sprung, as they say. But a girl I know might know." Suddenly haughty, he added, "What they *see* in him! Lukie too, a while back. Oh well, sex, forget it, no point trying to find any sense in it. Give me your number."

"I'm at my aunt's for the time being, here's hers." He wrote it on a cocktail napkin.

"But back to Nellie—I did like her, you know, a lot—and I haven't a clue if this has anything to do with her at all, except it stuck in my mind when I heard that whatever happened could have been around midnight." He hesitated. "This is dumb. You'll think I'm just trying to roll up a hundred and five dollars' worth of chat."

"Go ahead anyway."

"Believe it or not, I have some kind of principles. Anything I tell you I will *not* tell all over again to the police. In fact, for the record I never spoke to you at all."

"All right. Understood."

"Because this guy was really— Well. Close to twelve, a man came out of Twenty, sort of stumbling. People do stumble around here, at that hour, but he looked, that man, stunned and I think he was bent over so you couldn't see him sort of . . . gasping, or crying, or both. Big tall man, raincoat, pink face, I think dark hair, reminded me for some reason of a politician, maybe Hugh Carey, that kind of face."

It could have been anyone. It could have been Matthew, materializing before Jeremy's eyes, a ghostly Matthew swept with white and silver light.

"I thought for a moment he was going to fall down," Nix said. "He'd had it. One way or another, that man had had it."

Five

Perhaps it was just as well Matthew was not at home at ten minutes after ten.

And what would he have said to him if the telephone had been answered? Look here, Matthew, what made a public wreck of you around midnight, at 20 Timothy Street, just about the time Nellie was killed?

There must be thousands upon thousands of tall, pink-faced, dark-haired men in New York. There must be at least ten or twelve tenants living in Nellie's apartment building.

At any given hour in the city, there must be a man, or many a man, who had visibly had it. Upon whom loss, destruction, despair, had suddenly crashed.

It would be more than unfair to go to the police with Nix's snippet, which had at first hit him like a blow in the ribs but which with the passing minutes became shot full of questions, of uncertainties.

He decided to let it wait until he was face to face with Matthew. Preferably tomorrow. There was one obvious thing, though, to do right now. Call Ursula, and if she wasn't back from dinner yet—or if she was, and was being made love to by Sam Gamble—keep on calling until she answered.

She did answer immediately, and she sounded alone.

"Sorry to bother you, but I thought I'd relieve you of that box and I want to ask you something. Are you in bed?"

Ursula had been, but she said politely, "Reading. Yes, all right, Jeremy."

Entering 3A, he said, "I seem to have spent the day in your apartment. If you're not in bed you should be. You look shot."

The hall was small and they were very close to each other. She wore a soft blue robe and her hair was pleasantly loose around the shadowed pale face. He stood looking at her. Then he laid his hands on her shoulders, lightly. He put gentle lips to her temple, a feather touch of flesh that felt to both of them like a startling electric charge.

"Do you think you should be alone here tonight? After your . . . encounter?"

Nellie more or less left you to me. Well, I'll begin using my inheritance, then, Ursula put it to herself.

"If I had wanted company for the night it was more than available," she said. And then watching the sudden color sting his face, "But it's kind of you to be concerned." She moved away from his hands to open the closet door. "If I remember you put it on the right somewhere."

"I'll get it." He reached behind the sou'wester and his fingers closed unwillingly around the cool enameled metal. Not a time to linger, not with this ghastly small burden. Not in the face of a refusal which he found to his astonishment cut deep and hurt severely. "One quick thing. Did Matthew come around visiting you here on Saturday night, latish? Or leave late, that is, about twelve?" Matthew was, after all, her cousin by marriage.

The question seemed to come from far away and to make no sense whatever. Her mind was on an enormous voyage, into the future, into nowhere. Had she just managed the single most self-defeating gesture of her lifetime? The proud rejection probably final? It never really started and now it's over. Period.

"Matthew? Saturday night? I'm sounding stupid but I don't follow you." You could have been following me, into the living room, into the bedroom.

Oh but—the hot blood swept not only her face but her whole body. His intention for the night, thoughtful and protective, might have been the wing chair he found so comfortable in Sam's presence, or the sofa. And she had, oh God, leaped to the assumption that what he had in mind was making love. Unhand me, sir! Oh *God.*

She had the strangest feeling that his hands were still on her shoulders, even though they were where they belonged, at his sides.

Deliberately vague—don't spell out for her what might be a

terrible accusation—he said, "I was just trying to piece things together, I gather he didn't visit you then."

"No. I haven't seen him for weeks." She felt she should be at least as nice to him as he had been to her, verbally. "You must have had about five days in one, today. Shouldn't you take a little time off from whatever you're doing upstairs, and go to bed yourself?"

"Yes, not a bad idea. Good night, Ursula."

She thought she had a faint glimmer of whatever he was doing, upstairs, when on Wednesday morning with her coffee she made her way through the New York *Times*.

"Jeremy." There was a schoolmistress rap in Enid's voice on the telephone. "I ask, I demand, that you come here right away. My back has given up. I am at home. I am in bed. I must see you."

"I'm just making coffee. Give me fifteen minutes, Enid."

It was a little after nine o'clock. He had had a heavy sleep induced by the powerful drug of total mental and bodily fatigue. At first he resisted the idea of sleeping in Nellie's bed but that was the starting step around some neurotic bend. And anyway, the sofa was just a foot or so away from the orange towel. Before going to bed he picked it up and put it in the garbage can; then scrubbed the rug with water and peroxide from a bottle he found in Nellie's medicine cabinet.

Enid's apartment, at which in the course of the years he had attended several parties, was on Waverly Place. It was small, crowded, and colorful, jammed with mementoes of the many lives she had led. She let him in, skin chalky, tangled gray hair in her eyes, but retaining her grande dame presence in spite of it, wearing an all-but-threadbare Chinese silk robe patterned with embroidered poppies and butterflies.

She put a long thin hand to the lapel and said, "Do pardon my past splendors, Jeremy. The bedroom, if you don't mind."

He followed her. She climbed into bed and leaned against lace-edged pillows. Over the elaborate brass headboard was a photograph of her with her first or second husband, Jeremy couldn't remember which. They both sat in camp chairs, in khakis and topis, guns resting against their chairs, long grass at their feet, a splendid dead lion lying in it.

She thrust her copy of the *Times* at him, folded to the weather page. She had looped his ad with savage red crayon. Her oval fingernail came pouncingly down on it.

"You must try to explain to me this obscene advertisement, or commercial notice, or whatever it is. 'Nellie lives. 20 Timothy Street. J.O.'" Her slender-lipped mouth was shaking as she recited it.

"I suppose you might call it a kind of memorial," Jeremy said. "Or a—"

She cut sharply across him. "It's shocking, outrageous. Do you —I *suppose* you're J.O.—belong to some odd cult I haven't been informed of? Is there some arcane ritual when one of you dies?"

"People," Jeremy said slowly, "don't disappear that fast, even when they're cremated. They leave all kinds of bits and pieces, unfinished business, things unsaid that were meant to be said, hanging in the air behind them. Things undone that were meant to be done."

"And this is Nellie clearing up these items from the grave? Or rather, from her blue box?" Enid reached for her cup of coffee on the bedside table. A strong scent of brandy floated from it.

He was silent, watching her sip. He considered her contemptuous questions rhetorical.

"It sounds to me," Enid went on, "more like some sort of veiled threat. Are you sure that isn't what you meant? Although why, and against whom—I don't imagine vicious sneak-thieves peruse the *Times*. Is this a one-time thing, or is it to be repeated?"

"Three times. In your word, a ritual kind of number."

"I consider it insulting if not insane. I consider it a desecration of Nellie's memory." As direct as he had always known her to be, she said, "I'm sorry to have troubled you. I don't think I want to know you any more, Jeremy. The connection between us has been severed, to say the least."

Her imperious tone summoned an invisible footman; he could almost hear, "Show the gentleman out."

"Sorry, Enid. I hope your back improves." At the bedroom door he paused and turned. Sunlight from the long window beside the bed struck him, making him look younger than he was, the eyes very dark, the fresh flashing wit all gone from them, and from his mouth. Younger and thinner and a little lost.

"One last thing," he said. "Do you know anyone who knew Nellie who wears pince-nez?"

Obviously taken aback by what seemed an inconsequential question, she said, "No. Pince-nez? Yes. Gretel's husband Robert. I met him once, which was more than enough."

"Thank you." He lifted a farewell hand and left her.

Gretel had no strong religious beliefs, but she had a gratified feeling that a deity, if not *the* Deity, had stepped in at the right time, financially speaking.

This was her husband Robert's first week at home as a man of leisure. Orion Enterprises, a chain of drug, clothing, and shoe stores of which he was an executive vice president, had fallen into a well of mismanagement and debt which, combined with consumer resistance to ever-mounting prices, put it into bankruptcy.

Robert had been with Orion for seventeen years. At his age, fifty-eight, he would find it very hard to match his status and his salary of sixty thousand a year.

They had known it was coming for months, Gretel and Robert, but Friday was a black day, the end of some kind of world. Having cleared his office and having had a grim drink with the president, he drove home to East Orange.

"I have lines out," he assured his wife. "It will just be a matter of time. We must be patient."

Gretel was not by nature a patient woman. She hadn't had to think about their bank balance for two decades. As a gesture of punishing economy, she cooked and served frankfurters and baked beans on Monday night. On Tuesday, Charles Lambert, Lise's lawyer and hers, called.

Wednesday morning, she was checking the weather in Charleston, South Carolina. It might be nice to have a little fling, take a short run down there to see her sister-in-law. Charleston was lovely, a mass of bloom, at this time of year. And she could let her sister-in-law share their good news.

The public and commercial notices column was to the right

of the temperature listings in the *Times*. Something drew her eye to a short insertion.

"*Nellie lives . . .*"

She was sitting in the breakfast nook in her sunny kitchen, having a celebratory third cup of coffee, although she usually only allowed herself two. Bad for the complexion.

There was a single great thump in her breast. She had telephoned Lise Monday evening to ask her how she was feeling, then inquired politely after Lise's friend Nellie.

"She's dead, murdered," said Lise, voice bruised. "She's gone." A steady empty buzz on the line.

Gretel found Robert at the desk in his study, obsessively going through papers taken from his attaché case. Keeping a slipping, sliding world in order, even though it now seemed that his wife had, after an eternity, arrived at the possession of her money. Filing in his deep right-hand drawer full of manila folders, A under A and B under B. "Getting squared away," he called it.

He looked up and said, "What's the matter? Not, please God, your heart again, Gretel?"

She placed the *Times* in front of him. "Look. Mad, isn't it? I mean—"

He read the notice twice, the second time out loud.

"Could Lise have been wrong?" Almost a whisper.

"Not about a thing like that," he answered harshly. "In any case—you can't trust Lise—I called the precinct station nearby and they said yes, she was. They wanted my name. I said a friend, John Morton, and then hung up."

"Why didn't you tell me?"

"I didn't want to worry you about morbid matters." He returned to his papers. "Besides, you hardly knew her."

"But this notice?"

"A form of mourning, I suppose. Your color is still very bad, Gretel. If I were you I would dismiss it from my mind."

Tranquilizers, double the daily amount allowed on the typed label, took Matthew through Sunday; Librium and a routine faithfully followed by him and Joy once a month, on separate Sundays.

He stayed in bed all day. It had been, originally, Joy's idea, the monthly blankout. "Just say to hell with everything for twenty-four hours. It not only renews the tissues and refreshes the skin but it's marvelous for all that litter lying around in your mind. It sort of flushes it away."

No newspapers, no books, no music, no television, went the routine. Rest, doze, sleep. At noon one brought the other a glass of sherry, and thin buttered toast and tea. After the somnolent afternoon, a long deep bath. And then back to bed, to a dinner tray of one martini, a cup of consommé, a broiled lamb chop, and chilled fresh fruit in wine.

It was an understood thing that no phone messages be passed along. Matthew heard the phone ringing dimly, and often, and twitched every time he did. Bringing in his lunch, Joy said, her eyes brilliant, "Everybody's heard. Everybody's calling up. I'm just noting down names for you. Naturally they all say more or less the same thing."

Monday had to be met and forded and was, magnificently. At 9 A.M. on every desk at UBC was a memo headed "To: ALL" from Brandon Benning, containing the press release on their new president, for publication in Tuesday's newspapers, and then a brief: "I am sure we will all wish him well." No unnecessary boat-rocking; a change of face, of name, business as usual, back to work, chums.

Tides of congratulation, a merry lunch fueled with drinks before, wine with the meal, his hosts the board of directors. In the afternoon, taking over the office at the top, immaculately emptied of another man's aura, ready to be filled with his. Torrents of phone calls, a glorious feeling of unreality that banished any and all other lines of thought.

Tuesday was jammed with briefing meetings. Tuesday was gotten through under outwardly full sail until he returned Jeremy Orr's call.

"I thought you might be able to help. I gather you were close to her. Your name was the next-to-last one I heard from her. Before it happened."

He was not given to reading classified ads in the *Times,* but Joy was. She called him from her office at ten on Wednesday. "Matthew, the strangest thing. I thought you might be able to figure out what it means," and read him the little insertion.

It was as though he had been waiting all along for it: this deadly plunging knife.

By Christ, he thought, I am not going to die three times. Twice is enough.

Six

For a while, there were reassuring ordinary sounds. A phone call from Lise, Charmian's voice warm and sympathetic. ". . . and you have plenty of books to read? All right then, I'll see you a little later in the week." Vacuuming, distant, from the bedroom: Mrs. Falconer on her every-other-day cleaning stint. The radio turned on, popular music; Charmian had finally gotten over rock. "Lay your head upon my pillow . . ." "I'll never fall in love again . . ."

Walter had come home early, at four. He had been worried all day about her face at breakfast, her silence, her look of being somehow at an immense distance from him. Of course, Nellie Hand had only been cremated yesterday. It would take her a little time to get over it. Perhaps a good idea, tonight, to have dinner out, some place with lots of people to distract her, amuse her.

"Walter," said the tape. "I was going to write you a letter but why not use this ridiculous thing?" Her voice was low and hesitant. "What happened to Nellie sort of . . . made me realize that life is terribly short. Anything can happen to you. One minute you're here and the next, you aren't. It's very selfish, but somehow every day now seems much more precious than it was." She paused, the pause before a plunge. "I'm going away for a few days, to think things over, to think about our lives . . . and mine . . . and what I want to do with mine. I won't tell you where, but you mustn't worry. Oh, that's silly, of course you'll worry. But it's something I absolutely have to do, I've been pulled every which way for a couple of months now. Do take care. I'll see you soon."

Silence. No vacuuming, music off. The very faint and final sound of a closing door.

He sat for a time listening to the whisper of the empty tape, willing it to give him the sound of the door opening again, the laughing breathless apology, "I don't know what got *into* me . . ."

Of course not. If she'd come back she'd be here now. He made himself figure this out, patiently. He went to her closet and found her small suitcase gone. The bedroom was tidy, no feel of Charmian around, no robe tossed on a chair, slippers kicked off, open book on the bedside table, perfume in the air.

She would probably be in the city somewhere; she was not a country person. Hardly staying with friends, as he could make a systematic tour of their friends' apartments. In a hotel, perhaps under another name. Or in an apartment where she knew she would be alone.

He went back a few tapes, mentally. "The painters are coming tomorrow. May I take shelter in your place? I know I have a key somewhere . . ."

The painters. They weren't due until a week from today, but he supposed he could have forgotten to tell her about the changed date.

Could she bear to stay in a place where the violent death of a dear friend had so recently, so freshly occurred? Yes, was his fierce answer to himself. Yes, if there was a man with her, and total privacy was essential. Pulled every which way for a couple of months. Whether to stay with her husband, or leave him for this other man?

He walked very fast to Timothy Street. Listening outside 4B, he was not reassured by the silence. Arms around her, mouth to mouth, what noise would that make? And then brisk footsteps inside, the door opening, a man—was it the man?

He recognized Nellie's nephew. Jeremy Orr, the look in whose eyes had nothing to do with dalliance, with happiness. Of course, the only relative, things to be done here—

"I'm afraid the money, the thirty thousand dollars in round numbers, is gone."

He thought for a second he was going to faint. The money must have been in the desk, held there for this moment, this flight. Must get away, mustn't let this man see what was happening to him, what ax had fallen cruelly upon his neck. And some madman with bagpipes blocking his way—

The dreadful emptiness of his apartment regained, he walked the living-room floor for an hour. Couldn't notify the police. "My wife has left me, will you try to find her and bring her back?" Couldn't call any of their friends; she might change her mind, she might be back tomorrow morning, or even late tonight. "Is Charmian with you? Do you know where she might be?" Poor jealous Walter, he must think she's up and left him. And his after-all groundless panic would be carved forever for them, in marble.

At ten o'clock he made himself eat a handful of crackers and drink a glass of milk. He went back over his tapes, playing segments at random, listening for the faintest hint, clue. But after a while he thought the sound of her voice would drive him crazy. His ears were ringing and his head ached horribly.

The desk. He must go through that desk. Nellie: "If there are any old diaries or love letters tied up in ribbons I promise not to read them."

And she might, by now, be there. Jeremy Orr would probably have gone home after completing his grim duties for the deceased.

Wait. If it was at all possible. Wait until morning. At a little before three he took one of her sleeping pills, rarely used by her; she had left the bottle behind. She wouldn't need sleeping pills. Not with him, the man.

He was appalled to find that it was almost ten o'clock when he woke. He called his office and told his secretary he would not be in today: family business. He called Nellie's number and waited through twenty rings. Naturally, she wouldn't answer the phone, unless by some prearranged signal. "Let the phone ring three times, hang up, wait one minute and then call again."

Disliking to have to look at his face in the mirror, he shaved, then showered and dressed. Not for him the hastily pulled-on trousers and any old off-duty top. A suit of a gray so dark as to be almost black, a white shirt, a black silk twill tie, an unconscious effect as of one about to attend a funeral. Complete with umbrella.

He knew Basil slightly and disapproved of him, but Basil at this point might be of use. Sitting on the front step of No. 20, the Russian was consuming his mid-morning prune Danish and coffee laced with vodka.

Walter bade him good morning and, wasting no time or words, said, "I wonder if you have a key to Nellie's apartment. Charmian's desk is there and she wants something out of it."

Basil delicately fingered prune filling from the corner of his mouth. "As a matter of fact I have. When she's away I feed George and when I'm away she feeds Lenin."

Following him up the stairs, Walter thought, oh God, I forgot the police lock, or seal, or whatever it is. I'll be on one side of the door, she'll be silently on the other.

But the lock had been removed. "In view of the circumstances," Basil said, "I feel it is my duty to attend you."

It was one of those mornings peculiar to New York in spring, a sinister dark gray-pink light, surging clouds hanging low, periods of untimely twilight causing headlights to be switched on. Rain threatened, thunder rumbled; the air was so still and so heavy with moisture that its pressure induced a feeling of ominous matters in store.

Jeremy had just removed the roll of film from his Minolta and put it in the pocket of his suitcase when he heard the key in the lock. For a second he felt an odd sensation, physical fear. But wasn't this what his tenancy here was all about?

Basil came confidently in, Walter with his haggard face and tightly rolled black umbrella behind him. Registering mild surprise, Basil looked at Jeremy, and then at the empty cup and newspaper and camera on the coffee table.

"I am sorry, I had no idea you were still here," he said. "Surely, my dear fellow, it would be wise to remove yourself from these premises? It can only feed one's grief—Nellie here, Nellie there, Nellie everywhere about you."

"Have you come up here—both of you—to attend to my emotional well-being?"

They stood two feet from him. Basil was his height, but chunkier, heavily muscled. Walter was taller and from him Jeremy got an impression of violence just barely under control. There was a curious silence and then Walter, looking down at his umbrella, said, "Well, the desk, you know, from last evening, when we were interrupted. And—my wife is often here, she's careless about leaving little things behind her. Do you mind if I take a . . . final look around?"

"No, go ahead. And Basil—you won't be needing that key any more."

Basil surrendered it gracefully. "It will no longer be necessary now that George has—at least I hope he has—a new owner, someone to take care of him."

Walter went to the desk and with uncertain hands filled his attaché case, leaving behind only the costume jewelry, the gloves, and a dozen old copies of Playbill. If she were here I think I could smell her, her skin and hair, her perfume, he thought; but she may be in collusion with Orr, he may be covering for her in some way.

Jeremy noted his eyes hungrily raking the living room as he said, "Just a quick check in the bedroom, a scarf, rain boots, something like that—" He crossed the room and pulled the bedroom door almost closed behind him.

Sitting on the sofa arm, Jeremy fought a feeling of frustration. This was ridiculous. Two possible murderers, one intent perhaps on removing some small vital object, the other planted in perfect self-possession on Nellie's slipper chair. While he did absolutely nothing about either of them.

Voice low, conversational, he said to Basil, "Did Nellie know about you? About the very special dittoes in your gallery?" Any measure, however bold, to break out of this glue of inaction.

Basil raised his eyebrows. "And I killed her because she did? Honorable lady that she was, she was about to inform on me? If I had, you'd be in danger yourself. Wouldn't you." The last two words a statement.

The livid light in the room darkened; Basil's back was to the window and his features could not be read.

"We have a witness at present."

"The witness will in time remove himself. To continue what I can only suspect is a hunt for a missing wife."

Then he laughed. "Academic, my dear Orr. I'm just an innocent bystander, a spotless copyist—although I'm flattered at whatever you're hinting. If you can prove otherwise, I shall be quite astonished."

No matter what you think you know, my dear Orr, I can guarantee to provide you with a dead end. Look high, look low, there are no stolen paintings in the gallery, never were and never will be.

Basil moved lazily, got up, put a hand on Jeremy's shoulder. Rain suddenly dashed itself against the window behind him. Almost tenderly, he said, "Yes, follow my advice, get out of this haunted place." As though to distract a man ill and incapable, he picked up the Minolta in its zipped leather case. "I've never used one of these. How many exposures on a roll does this infant offer?"

"Thirty-two. But it's empty."

"How out of character for a man like you. An eyeless camera. Like a photographer," he added thoughtfully, "who for some frightful reason loses his sight."

Walter came out of the bedroom. "Nothing." The single word had a desolate sound. "Nothing of Charmian's here. But thank you, Jeremy. Thank you, Basil."

Jeremy took the sudden unconsciously shielding hand away from in front of his eyes.

This was no time for delicacy toward a man to whom something not at all good had obviously happened.

"Nellie would have wanted Charmian to have her books," he said, not bothering with chapter and verse of this offhand bequest. "I'd like to talk to her anyway. Is she at home?"

"She's away," Walter said carefully. "Right now, that is. I'll have Jove collect the books with the desk. Very kind of you." He left in haste as if he wanted no more observation of his face, his voice.

"Now then, Jeremy." Basil effortlessly assumed the role of father. His brown eyes sparkled with sympathy under the thorny brows. "No matter what, you can't bring Nellie back. My advice to you is to let bygones be bygones."

A threat? Something arranged to happen to your eyes?

"Let's see, what do I know about you, what do I guess? Income of probably close to eighty thousand a year, net. Most of your working life spent with beautiful if stupid women." He was counting off these points on his fingers.

"That commodious estate on Thirty-first Street, princely quarters, in this city. Oh, and Ursula, who seems to burst into flames whenever you appear on the scene. A lot to lose."

"I don't see the connection. Lose?"

"That is, if *you* choose to lose yourself, bury yourself in some obsession. Are you sure that with these mysteries and pursuits of yours—'Nellie lives'"—a snort of laughter—"you haven't Russian blood somewhere? Connivers all, thinks the Russian."

Under the amusement, the outpouring of words, what he is saying, Jeremy thought, is *drop the bone*.

Was some sort of bargain being proposed? Leave me alone, I'll leave you and your life and Ursula alone.

An out-of-work and out-of-temper model had set a disastrous fire at his friend Dick Temple's studio eleven months ago.

Forget it, he seemed to read between Basil's lines. Even if I do fiddle pictures. Even if I—

"Think about it," Basil counseled. "I must leave you. Someone may be pounding at my door for a Rembrandt."

Why, anyway, was he doing this, pursuing this? Would it be wiser to leave Nellie in her box?

He went into the hall and looked up at the blue-enameled object on the shelf. As at Ursula's, a hall, at a slight remove from actual living quarters, seemed the only appropriate place for such a thing.

A box. Perhaps five by five by five inches. Nellie.

He was eaten with a rage he knew would never burn itself out if he left her there, consumed, unexplained, and forgotten.

Seven

Hearing the feet approach her landing and then continue on up, Ursula went to her door and quietly opened it. Neither man looked back to discover her inquiring gaze.

What was Walter Lyle doing away from his executive chores at Intercoastal Petroleum? What errand pried Basil out of his gallery?

Wearing a faint self-derisive smile, she decided anyway that it might be a good idea to stand just inside the slightly open door, and listen, and wait. For what? The crash of a body hitting the floor? Knives though don't make any noise. Oh, for God's sake, Ursula.

After ten minutes, Walter Lyle came down the stairs, and after twelve minutes, Basil.

Surely Jeremy would be all right up there. Odd, however, the defeated droop of Walter's head and shoulders; odd, Basil's mirthless taut grin.

She went to the phone, called Nellie's number and three times in a row got a busy signal. Was he calling the police? Or a doctor? This is what happens, she told herself, when you let go of the everyday, when you live inside someone else in a mad sort of fantasy.

How many men were there in New York who wore pince-nez? Or to narrow it down, how many men who wore pince-nez would have contact, social or otherwise, with Nellie?

He called Lise. "I hope I didn't get you up, and I'll make it brief—do you know if your brother-in-law, Robert, is it?—would have any reason to pay a visit to Nellie Saturday night?"

Lise had already been called by an outraged Enid: "If you haven't seen page twenty-one in your *Times*, take a look. That young man Jeremy seems to have gone demented overnight, and is playing some kind of game of hide-and-seek in the public prints."

Lise had leadenly accepted the bloody hand of careless fate which had extinguished Nellie; but she was an intriguer to her bones.

"It's nice to hear your voice, there's something of Nellie in it. Lower of course. But what's this about Robert?"

"Just a blind guess. Met her about nine thirty Saturday night outside and went in with her, took her arm although she seemed not very happy about his company. Pince-nez, homburg, gray hair, middle fifties. I thought it was likely that it was someone she knew."

Lise leaped on the chance to torture Gretel and Robert.

"I don't know anything about it, but I'll find out."

She finished her coffee in relishing gulps and dialed her sister in East Orange. Without preliminary, she said, "What was Robert doing at Nellie's Saturday night more or less around the time she was killed?"

There was a stunned pause. Then, breath found, "I haven't the vaguest idea what you're talking about."

"I see it all," Lise said with savage glee. "Don't think I don't know about your scurrilous attack on Nellie. She gave me a nice kind expurgated version but I can well hear every word you said. She actually asked me to think twice about naming her, but of course I told her that was out of the question. So what have we now, hmmm?" Her turn to pause. "So Robert decides to take over the persuasion, and the threats, thinking the male command is more effective than the female."

"You're mad. But that's nothing new."

"And Nellie resisted, and he lost his temper. It's almost as bad as yours when you do, finally, let go. Maybe threatened her, shook her— Say she was in the kitchen and picked up a knife to defend herself. He snatched it from her. Quick, *quick.* Annoying heir disposed of. Then mess up the apartment. Make off with a couple of things, easy. Especially to someone as efficient and coolheaded as Robert."

"I would tell you exactly where Robert was Saturday night

—and what television show we were watching together. Except that I will not lower myself to do so."

"No one—the police, that is—ever pays any attention to a wife's testimony. I feel it my duty to notify them immediately about this visit. Good-bye, Gretel."

She called Jeremy back, mouth curved in a baleful grin. "Swears she knows nothing about it, that he was home watching television. I know she's lying in her teeth, and scared. Shall I call the police or will you?"

The delighted malice in her voice came clearly along the wire. "Think of it, proper Gretel, a police car arriving under her East Orange porte cochere. Husband taken away for questioning in a murder case. These things get around. She'll never get over it. And there are always people who will say to each other, 'Did you know Robert Balham killed somebody but they could never prove it?'"

The blast of vengeance put Jeremy on his guard. He knew from Nellie the relationship between the two sisters; it had amused his aunt. Lise would inevitably announce that Gretel was lying.

"And he'd just lost his big-money job, he'd be in a mood to be anxious about the future," Lise added triumphantly. "Now. About the police?"

"Let it wait a bit." There wasn't enough here, to join Lise in her thirsty clawing spring on her brother-in-law. "The police think they have a line on their man."

For the first time he found himself wishing that Tost would turn out—in spite of all his instincts to the contrary—to be the one who had killed Nellie.

Ursula was about to try to reach Jeremy for the fourth time when her own phone rang. Joy Jones said, "I thought I'd never make a connection. Don't you ever hang up?" An invitation: would Ursula like to join her for a couple of days at the beach house in Amagansett? The weather was supposed to clear by midafternoon. She, Joy, was going to get the place spruced up and lay in supplies for weekends, but Ursula, she said, could lounge about and soak up salt air.

Ursula said instantly, with relief, "Yes, I'd love to." Leave this, all of it. She was caught up on her work at least through Friday. Fine, Joy would pick her up in the car at around noon. "You won't mind if I write releases for Troy Motor Company over drinks?"

One small thing to do first, before welcome flight. Do it in person. She went up the stairs for three reasons. Burning curiosity unadmitted, possibly helpful contribution admitted. And at the back of her mind the cloudy and last-minute intention of somehow retrieving her life, not acknowledged or examined at all.

When he opened his door, she said, "Good morning, I'm glad to see you're well and thriving."

"Come in, Ursula. How did you think you'd find my condition?"

Walking into the living room, she said to the air, " 'Nellie lives.' Freely translated, the question of who killed her, what sort of death it was, is not neatly docketed. I, J.O., her nephew, know certain things no one else could know. If you think what I know might be dangerous to you, and if you want to do anything about it, here I am, at Twenty Timothy Street. All alone. Beckoning you."

She hadn't until now spelled it out so thoroughly to herself. Shaken, she turned and faced him.

"At least, that's the way it reads to me. Otherwise there would be no point in the notice. Unless some kind of tribute . . . but that's not your style."

"How do you know my style on such brief acquaintance? But then of course, you would." He moved to her and put his arms lightly around her.

Trying to look as if this was the way any two people might casually converse, Ursula said hastily, unable to keep her eyes off his near and faintly smiling mouth, "I don't know if it's any use to you but—" Wasn't there anything she could do about her hot betraying skin? Two inches, one— He kissed her, delicately, lips lingering and moving over hers. Not aching lonely need, this time. Deliberate claiming power took over.

Push him away, don't kiss him back . . . and *again*. How sweet and strong, his mouth and body, how dazzlingly unfamiliar and yet known somewhere in flesh and bone.

He lifted his head. He looked bemused, eyes half-closed.

"Where . . . was I?" she murmured.

"You had gotten as far as 'but.' I'd better, for concentration's sake, let you go. For the moment."

She hardly knew what she was saying. All right, so the man's attracted to you. For the moment. Get on with it. "Matthew was here Saturday around six. He pressed my buzzer by mistake, and he couldn't have been coming to visit anybody but Nellie. As he might be one of the last people she talked to before it happened, she might have said something to him. About why she was afraid to stay here and wanted to go to your place for the rest of the weekend."

How quickly, she thought, he collected himself; she felt the sharply focused interest, now of quite another kind.

"Strange he didn't say so when I talked to him. Why wasn't he at the service for her, by the way?"

"I didn't think to call him. I was barely functioning." Just as I am barely functioning now.

"Don't say you told me. And stay out of this from here on in. I want you"—moving again, he slid his hands from her shoulders over her breasts to her waist and held them there—"intact."

"And naturally," voice calm enough but why the ache of tears in her throat? "I want you intact, Jeremy. Don't get hurt. Please."

He kissed her temple and let her go. He sighed. "This is no place for love," he said.

She put a tentative butterfly hand to his cheek and he covered it with his own.

"I'm going off for a couple of days, to Long Island. I must go and pack a few things now."

"Good. But give me the number. I must have you on hand one way or another."

She found the Amagansett number in her small green address book. Wanting not to leave him, especially now, she said again as they went hand in hand to the door, "Please, Jeremy—"

"Please Jeremy *what?*" He bent to her, laughing a little, close and owning.

"Please Jeremy dear—don't, don't get hurt."

"If I'm to be overlooked and temporarily forgotten I'd rather it was because of music than oil and gasoline," Charmian said. But Victor, intent on his piano, didn't hear her.

His apartment was on Riverside Drive, with a great rain-swept view of the Hudson, in what had become an unfashionable and dangerous neighborhood. But it had lofty ceilings and many rooms, halls, nooks, bays, the pleasure of generous and unexpected spaces. He had collected the furniture and ornaments and Chinese rugs himself.

He was at thirty-nine a successful composer, with a movie score every year or so to round out his professional income. But he had always had money of his own, left by his parents. Which, Charmian thought, might have been one of the reasons why he was so delightfully languid, unrushed, given to slowly savoring the moment.

"I'm transposing you into music," he said over his shoulder. A runnel, a ripple on the piano, crystal-silver sounding at the top, warm and soft on the lower keys. Raising his voice, "I'm enjoying our wedding trip here but how soon are you going to tell Walter?"

She came and sat on the piano bench beside him. She kissed him under the ear. "I would do the decent thing and tell him face-to-face but I think perhaps he might try to kill me."

"Yes, I worry about you, but then I worry about me," Victor said in lazy self-preservation. "Does he know who I am? I'm not in the phone book, so no address available, but still—"

"You are V.L. in my diary. Back then, when I was young," Charmian explained wistfully, "initials looked secret and romantic." They had had a brief love affair when she was in her mid-twenties, had met again two months ago at a party, started a flicker, and found a fire. "But Walter never comes up this way. It's an out-of-date part of town, and there are no corporations around."

Victor Laver lifted his hands from the piano. "One thing. This business of your unfortunate friend Nellie—you don't think by any chance Walter had anything to do with it? You don't think he knew I was there with you on Friday? or was told by someone I was? Mull it over while I get us some champagne."

Charmian didn't want to mull it over. She had been circling around the subject since Sunday, when Nellie was found, but deliberately getting no nearer the unthinkable center.

He'd pick up on the tape, of course, the business about the

painters coming Friday. Silly of her, the date had been changed and they wouldn't be coming for a week. But the excuse had just rushed out of her mouth, a reason to give Nellie so that she and Victor could have the apartment to themselves; an innocent and clear explanation to Walter as to where she had spent her day.

He hadn't questioned her about the painters. Perhaps he hadn't gotten around to that tape yet. Could he have gone Saturday, after she was in bed and asleep, to see Nellie? And having been unable to get any information from her—information which she did not have—flown into one of his rages? Seeing Nellie as conspirator, procurer?

She remembered a lamp smashing into the fireplace a year ago, a thousand-dollar emerald-green chiffon Stavropoulos dress ripped from throat to hem because a man at a wedding reception liked her too much in it.

Victor came back with the champagne. A slender fair man, with a supple face and surprising dark blue eyes under the careless fall of glossy hair across an elegantly boned brow. On some impulse of loyalty, she said, "No, I don't think it was Walter."

As he poured, holding the two glasses in one hand, the other, bottle-wielding arm around her, she began softly to weep.

"It's appalling," she whispered against his comforting lips. "It's hideous, that in a way Nellie had to die for me to be so happy."

Eight

This will put an end to it one way or another, Matthew told himself on the way downtown in a taxi.

His secretary had fielded two calls today from Jeremy Orr. Matthew had pulled up the blanket of business over his head and was not available.

"Sorry, Mr. Orr, a dozen people are trying to get hold of him, and there's a United Nations lunch that will probably stretch."

And, "No, there's no point in your coming up here, Mr. Orr, it would just be a waste of your time. A dinner meeting, and then a screening of a new pilot. Aren't I dumb, but I finally realized who you are—you're the *photographer.*"

It wasn't mere childish putting off on Matthew's part. It had to be dark, in case things didn't go well and reassuringly. He called Jeremy just before the screening, which was perfectly genuine, and said, "We've got to talk. I must say I'm fascinated by your 'Nellie lives.' I have some ideas of my own. Would nine thirty or so suit you? Down there?"

He had with him in his attaché case a gun, but only for his own protection if it was necessary; a nine-foot length of No. 10 nylon rope; and a long white silk muffler.

He did a quick mental review of Nellie's apartment, and its surroundings on the courtyard side, where the fire escape was. Directly across from her back windows was a restaurant on the ground floor fronting on Timothy Street with, as far as he could remember, offices above, a beauty shop, a real estate agency, both probably closed at this hour. To the left, the dingy rear of a garage. On the fourth side, a mean narrow five-story dwelling with a vertical row of small blind frosted-glass bathroom windows. Conveniently without eyes, the cobblestoned courtyard.

How bitter, how comfortable it would be to lay it out for

Jeremy exactly as he thought it was. To say, I didn't kill her
but I had every intention of doing so. I went up the stairs
to kill her and the door was open and— In my upbringing, Catholic you know, the will is tantamount to the deed, the guilt is
the same. If she hadn't been dead I would have gone right ahead.
I think.

In any case, you can see her death is on my hands.

I died with Cox and I died with her and by God I'm not going
to die with you.

One chance in ten there might be nothing in it at all. Just a
brief conference about what Orr evidently considered the unsolved mystery of Nellie's murder. And an old friend of hers
called upon for ideas, for help, for some kind of pointer.

One chance in ten that it would turn out that now and forever
he was free and could own himself once more. Throw himself
headlong into the worries and rewards and excitements of power.
Take a long easy breath, secure at the top.

It's just conscience that makes you think the newspaper message was directed, solely and simply, to you. With the hope that
you will do what you are doing now: head, in the busy golden-
dazzled darkness, for Timothy Street.

Surely not risky. One or the other might have been responsible,
but certainly not both. If one was dangerous, the other was safe
to have around. And there was a certain grim pleasure in setting up the second man as emergency guard.

At nine o'clock, Jeremy went down the stairs and rang the bell
at the door of Basil's apartment, halfway down the corridor leading to the rear entrance. Aware that he was being studied
through the eyehole, he said, "I come in peace, Basil, more or
less."

"*Entrez,*" Basil said, leading the way into his stage-set living
room. "Lonely upstairs, all by yourself?"

He wore a creamy embroidered raw silk smock over his corduroys, had a drink in his hand, and looked very much at ease.

"I have an odd request to make of you. I'm expecting a visitor
who may turn out to be one way or another an unknown quantity. Do you think you might drift up the stairs at, say, nine forty-
five or so to borrow a cup of sugar?"

Basil's eyes sparkled. "At the price of sugar, I'd be delighted. I can throw in a bonus if you like. Lenin—my cat—likes an occasional visit with George. Runs up the fire escape. I might go looking for him on and off. The view is quite good over the top of the cafe curtain."

"Good. I'll expect you, in both places."

"A little vodka?"

"No thanks."

"You must," Basil said gravely. "We are both making some kind of bargain, some kind of pledge, are we not?"

Their eyes met. "Yes, a little vodka," Jeremy said, and quickly downed an icy two fingers.

After the climb back up to Nellie's, he stood warily in the center of the room looking around him. Fireplace furniture, a long-handled hearth brush, tongs, a poker. The wine-bottle lamp seen through the kitchen door, good long neck to grip. The lamp suddenly reminded him of Ursula struggling in Tost's arms.

A heavy, green, oblong ceramic box on the coffee table, meant for cigarettes but as he had found filled with mismatched buttons, safety pins, and folded clipped-out newspaper and magazine recipes. He lifted it up and put it down.

He had no clear idea of what he expected from Matthew's visit. "I have some ideas of my own." Perhaps some seeming scrap or fragment, some significant recollection on Matthew's part. A door opened, something to get a toe into.

Perhaps—and a fantastic *perhaps* it was—a killer come to deal with this impudent interfering nephew of Nellie's. But he would probably not, in the fantasy, take any action here and now. Another body in Nellie's apartment to cope with. And not an obscure Village saleslady this time, but a man upon whom, dead, a very bright spotlight would shine.

He was a civilized man not given at any time to physical violence and his survey of possible weapons produced a peculiar feeling under his ribs.

Hurry, Matthew. Don't be late or Basil may turn up with his empty cup and you might not get around to whatever it is you're coming here to talk about.

Matthew arrived a little after nine thirty. "Evening, Jeremy." Obviously tired, eyes pouched, but pink and vital-looking, his presence was large in the room. Cold damp April air wafted from him as he stripped off his trench coat and threw it over a straight chair. He placed his attaché case on the floor beside the chair.

So as not to have to turn his back to his guest in the kitchen, Jeremy had put a bottle of scotch, ice, and glasses on the coffee table.

"Sit down and have a drink, Matthew."

Matthew roved the living room, looked into the kitchen, wondering if possible witnesses, listeners, were tucked away somewhere?

"If you'll excuse me, I can't for the moment sit, I've been sitting all day and through dinner and after dinner. God, that pilot! 'The Cheerybye Girls.' Four high school cheerleaders and their lives and loves and their bobbing breasts! I must say you're a braver man than I am, Jeremy; how the *hell* can you stand this place? Surrounded by her. I swear she's still here."

"Yes, she is," Jeremy said. "In a box on the closet shelf. Her ashes."

Matthew broke into a sweat and visibly forced himself to sit down in the slipper chair. Jeremy reached across from his place on the sofa and handed him a drink.

"What exactly,"—after a long pull on his glass—"did you or do you mean by 'Nellie lives'?"

"I meant that she didn't carry all her inside information about her friends safely into the flames." His voice was deliberately hard and provocative.

Leaning forward, Matthew said, "I know the state of shock after a horribly important death in your life. I've been there myself. But do you still really think—now, at a little distance—that it was faked and someone she knew killed her?"

His tone was one of patience, kindness; and the hint of age and experience to steady this younger man who had gotten this madly buzzing bee in his bonnet.

"I do." No point now in qualifying the answer.

"Well then, I have an idea, as I told you over the phone. Suppose a ten-thousand-dollar reward was offered for information leading to the discovery of—of whoever. Money will do things that police work alone can't do. I'd split it with you."

Jeremy thought he heard a switching of voice, from the efficient and executive to the naked and private. "I don't want to go on wondering for the rest of my life, either—if you're by any chance right—which of her friends killed Nellie Hand."

"That's very generous of you, Matthew," Jeremy said. "And I don't want to go on wondering for the rest of my life why you were here twice on Saturday, once around six and the next time around midnight."

He hadn't thought his way to this. The words came out on some furious switched-on tape over which it seemed he had no control. "And why you looked, according to my observer, wrecked—like a man, he said, who had had it."

He had thought some kind of attack possible, and thought himself well prepared for it. But he had not counted on the open savagery he had evoked.

Matthew hurled his full glass in his face, stepped up on the coffee table, and from this height flung his one hundred and ninety-five pounds on Jeremy, who, half-blinded with scotch and water, was trying to get to his feet.

Breath forced from his body, pinioned, on his side, trying to raise a knee, he was shoveled to the floor and before waking muscles and partly recovered breath could come to his aid was struck hard by a heavy skillful fist.

Basil, cup in hand, had just arrived outside the door of 4B when he heard the great thud and the strangled cry. He ran down the stairs and out the back entrance and began, at a slower speed, up the fire escape.

Helping an acquaintance obviously being subjected to violence of some kind—if he hadn't instituted it himself—was all very well, but there was his own neck to think of.

It would be wise to proceed silently, and in no great hurry, upward, to assess exactly what he was letting himself in for.

Close against the building wall outside Ursula's unlighted windows, he paused and listened, eyes on Nellie's window with its heavy protective screen.

The screen swung inward. A big man climbed out and swiftly knotted a rope over the fire-escape rail. He leaned in again over the sill, lifting, heaving, and in the faint light Basil saw Jeremy Orr's unresisting body hauled out.

Basil, as motionless, as cold as though encased in ice, watched the fumbling hurried hands looping the rope over his victim's head.

"*Look here!*" Basil bellowed. "You can't do that! There are four men right behind me—"

An endless second. An absolute stillness above him. Then Jeremy's upper body, released, hit the iron railings with a thump and the big man went back in through the window.

Four floors might not be high enough. The roof.

Matthew ran up the final flight of stairs and wrestled with the rusted knob. The door lurched suddenly open, almost knocking him down the stairs.

The water tower with its narrow steel ladder was just barely discernible in the darkness. As he climbed it, he thought, this tower, these rungs, this is where I've been heading all my life, this was always my destination. Or almost my destination.

There was a distance of perhaps seven feet from the base of the tower to the low parapet of the roof. Matthew leaped out and over and down, screaming, to the courtyard.

Basil, finding pulse and heart functioning, left Jeremy where he was for the moment and went in through the window and called the police. He saw the trench coat on the chair, the attaché case open on the floor beside it, and the open front door. Sensing the emptiness of the apartment, feeling that it had been fled from, he nevertheless planned to take the Colt .32 from the case after he delivered his message. With a shock of insight, he gathered that the white silk muffler had not been needed for its possible use.

"Man just tried to kill another man, hang him from the fire-escape railing here. No, he's alive, but I have no idea what shape he's in—oh Jesus *Christ—*"

The awful torn scream, the decisive thumping crash down below, down in the courtyard. "I think, for God's sake can you get somebody here right away—I think he's just killed himself."

Jeremy calculated later that he had been out not more than six or seven minutes.

He opened his eyes to the overcast night sky and felt the iron uprights of the fire-escape railing hard against the back of his head, pressing against a fury of pain. Something at his throat—he fingered and then dimly saw the rope, the noose.

He removed it, tried to get to his feet, succeeded after several seconds, and then became aware of the shouting and confusion below. People gathering, a door swinging open, the back door of No. 20, to let out a flood of light on something sprawled face down on the cobblestones.

For a ghastly moment he wondered if, conscious without knowing he was conscious, he had somehow heaved Matthew over the edge of the fire escape in a final life-or-death struggle.

But the noose, to hang him with. He saw the thick workman-like knot on the rail, and the slack length of four or five feet before the rope had been looped.

Not wanting to go down the fire escape to the thing, the sprawl in the court, not even able to on uncertain legs, he got himself through the window. One knee felt as if Matthew's stunning collapse from above might have broken it. But no, in that case, it wouldn't merely be agonizing; it wouldn't work at all.

Basil, back from the courtyard, found him in the bathroom, bent slightly swaying over the toilet, retching miserably but to no effect. He handed him a paper cup of water drawn from the washbasin faucet. Jeremy, face distorted, eyes suffused with blood, drank it down and gave his head a hard clearing shake. On a great gasping trembling breath, he straightened.

"What happened? Matthew's down there, isn't he."

Basil was looking pale and ill himself. "Wash your face, you're covered with vintage Village soot, and then a drink if you can swallow it. I know I can."

Pouring scotch, he regarded the slant of Nellie's sofa. "It's lost one of its legs."

"Amazing that it didn't go right straight through the floor," Jeremy said.

The straight whiskey restored Basil somewhat and kindled his love of drama. "I don't see it all, my dear Jeremy—drink, man, drink!—but I see some of it. You're not wanted around for some reason I can just vaguely fathom." He grinned briefly. "Hound dog after a possum, in your colorful American idiom. So, nephew now all alone in the world and overcome by grief—in short, while of temporarily unsound mind—takes his own life. Had been acting oddly, putting peculiar messages in the paper, couldn't tear himself away from the scene of the tragic death, wandered about the apartment trying to summon back his aunt— Yes. Very sound. And these talented successful artistic types can be most unstable."

Jeremy's eye lit on the open attaché case, the gun resting on a neat pile of papers. He got up, his legs now better able to support him, closed the case, and took it back with him to the crooked sofa.

Basil grinned again. "And who would blame you for being still a little nervous?"

The knocking at the door had an unmistakable authority: police.

A photograph of a handsome tall woman was found in Matthew's wallet; it was ventured that the woman might reasonably be his wife. The maid at the Joneses' Park Avenue apartment informed Sergeant Doehr of the Sixth Precinct that Mrs. Jones was staying at their beach cottage in Amagansett and supplied the number.

Ursula took the call as Joy was soaking in a hot tub after a strenuous afternoon.

The sergeant regretted to inform his listener that Mr. Matthew Jones had suffered a fall from a building, at 20 Timothy Street, and was dead, adding with an instinct of charity that death was immediate.

The hours after that always remained to her something of a blank. Joy getting out of the tub as the bathroom door was opened, the single scream, the sag, Ursula just managing to catch her wet slippery body.

Joy, terrible in her tearlessness, refusing tranquilizers, refusing brandy. "We must get back and I must drive. You said you'd let your license lapse. I'll probably—oh God—be wanted for identification. Pack your own things while I have some coffee. I'll just leave everything of mine here until the next weekend we—" And then the blank frozen stare as realization poured over her. There wasn't a "we" any more.

The night drive into Manhattan, too fast, seventy-five, eighty, but they weren't stopped by police. Silence. Nothing to say. No comfort to offer, no snatched-at platitudes. A man in his prime, a man fresh on his summit. Matthew the conqueror.

At one red light, Joy said, "Fall? *Fall?* He's killed himself. Why, Ursula?"

Besides not at the time being able to think at all, Ursula didn't know Matthew well enough to offer a reason why. The obvious answer dimly presented itself: death sentence delivered by a doctor, kept secret from Joy.

At the apartment, Joy calling the Sixth Precinct again, a gray parody of the efficient woman of business. "They say tomorrow morning will be all right for the identification. At the morgue. The man was quite kind, said if I wasn't up to it close friends could do it. But I must. I must. You'll stay here tonight, Ursula? Please? In a way I would very much like to kill myself too. I suppose it's catching."

Jeremy's tale told to Inspector Calder, with a sergeant busily taking it down in shorthand, was a brief one as far as the immediate facts preceding the suicide went.

Basil took up where of necessity he left off, his world suddenly gone dark and silent. "My God, *that* was the noise then. Jones crashing down on you."

Clear among mysteries, the leap from the roof. It was perfectly if horribly understandable. An onlooker to report what had happened. Network president attempts life of well-known photographer at scene of recent unsolved murder, the newspapers would shout.

Calder had just the two mens' word for it, however. Nothing to say yet that one or both of them hadn't given Jones the push. He was shown the rope, still knotted to the rail, its noose swinging slightly in the night wind. Okay, anyone can tie a knot in a rope.

He was very aware, Calder, of the thunderous power the police were about, if in time convinced, to have to tangle with; the forces of money, of status, of no doubt top legal brains. For Christ's sake, the *president* of United Broadcasting. Dead and broken in a dingy Village courtyard, the body not four feet from a stinking row of garbage cans.

And that Russian fellow in his fancy smock. He favored Basil with a glum frown. Fine witness he'd make, describing the alleged villainies of a high and mighty corporation president.

To Jeremy, he said with weary belligerence, "But can you give me *one* good reason why Jones would try to kill you?"

"I thought I had. My aunt was everybody's confidante and I implied to him that she passed some of her little store along to me . . . presumably something from his past that absolutely must not be known by anybody else. He'd had second thoughts and killed her for it, and now here I was, and he was going to have to start all over again. And if you want to dismiss all that as theory, I pinned him down as coming out of the front door here, at midnight on Saturday."

"I suppose it's not impossible." Stubborn unwilling voice. "We're a long way from the truth though. If you people would only leave things to the police—"

Out of the corner of his eye he saw Basil's mocking smile.

And Jeremy, remembering Berenson's half-amused dismissal of the suggestion that all might not be as it appeared, and that it might be an idea to do a rundown of Nellie's friends, did not trouble to answer.

If Matthew had shown, by the slightest word, the most barely readable turn of voice or expression, an involvement of any kind in Nellie's death, he had intended to inform Berenson immediately.

But Matthew in a final manner had made this notification unnecessary.

Basil remained at Calder's request to undergo, along with Jeremy, an examination by the precinct's Dr. McQuaid. This was conducted in the bedroom as the technical team was now crowding the living room, flashbulbs blueing the air.

Jeremy was promised a lump on his skull, bruising, and general discomfort by McQuaid, but no bones had been broken, even at the bad place in his left ribs. His questioning—"Now tell me exactly how this man attacked you"—became exceedingly tiresome, but Jeremy knew what he was up to.

After he had departed, he said to Calder, "I assume he has gathered that neither I nor Basil is drugged, drunk, crazy, or all three."

"Routine," Calder said, getting up from his flowered cricket chair. "I'm off. You'll hold yourselves available, of course. If you'll both sign these preliminary statements . . . And I suppose I don't have to tell you not to talk to the press until we know just what we have here."

Upon his leaving, Basil yawned. "I will now go downstairs to my bed, my book, and my vodka. Are you going to stay in this benighted place?"

"Yes, until morning anyway." He was suddenly too tired to even contemplate the short trek uptown. "There's no way to thank you but I have a little token of my regard." He went to his suitcase in the bedroom closet, took out the tiny roll of film, and handed it to Basil. "Village views. As a resident, you might like to have them."

The technical team was very busy on the rooftop, where the marks of footsteps faintly discernible in the grime led to the ladder of the water tower. The marks were carefully shielded with plastic film. The ladder rungs were fingerprinted. Useful evidence: because in this section of this city of eight million, not one of the hundreds of people questioned had seen Matthew Jones leave the tower and fling himself away.

Nine

At seven in the morning Ursula heard Joy on the telephone. She herself had had only a few short snatches of sleep; there had been the very real fear that Joy might slip into the bathroom and help herself to a lethal handful of sleeping pills. No matter how ragged, how shrill her usually measured voice, it was reassuring to hear it.

She had been dreadfully braced for the task of accompanying Joy to the morgue for the formal identification of her husband's remains, but Joy wouldn't hear of it.

"Under no circumstances. Bobby Locke is on the way over. Matthew's best friend and mine too. He'll stay with me and take care of things in general."

"Then I'll be off home as soon as he gets here." Home. Upstairs, perhaps, Jeremy. In a world gone cold and very dark a secret warmth flooded her.

Bobby Locke turned out to be a large stout man with kind gray eyes and an air of strength and competence. Good hands to leave Joy in.

Climbing the stairs at Timothy Street, Ursula thought, Mustn't check him this early, he may still be asleep. But then he probably isn't here at all.

If he was, he would know all about Matthew. For the tenth time, she wondered why this of all buildings in New York had been chosen for his probable suicide. Useless to conjecture, though; he couldn't at the time have been selective and sane.

She tried to shower away the weary night, dressed, and dialed Nellie's number. It was answered immediately.

"Where are you?" He was as near-frantic as she had ever heard him. "I tried Amagansett last night, then your place, then the apartment uptown, and you seemed to be absolutely nowhere. Then this morning, busy line there, zero here—"

"Well, right now, here is where I am."

Click. Thirty seconds later he was down the stairs and in at the door and they were repairing themselves, tight and silent in each other's arms.

After a time he lifted his mouth from hers. "Will you come upstairs with me? I've been told to expect the police sooner or later."

"But you look—I don't know—in some way battered," she said in alarm. She had been too close to him to see it before. "What's happened to you?"

He took her hand and opened the door. "You catch me up and I'll catch you up," he said, and kissed her on the second step and the fifth, and on the landing.

The telephone was ringing as they went into 4B. It was Enid, who seemed to have forgotten that she didn't know him any more. "Jeremy! I've seen the paper. My God, is it true?"

"Yes, it's true—you mean Matthew."

"'Fell or pushed'—but why *Timothy* Street? What was he doing there? Have you any idea?"

"Not that I can go into at the moment," Jeremy said. Telling Enid would be roughly equal to a formal announcement to the press.

"I'm coming over. I cannot bear it, being alone in the face of all this tragedy. I'd intended anyway to offer to take care of the disposal of Nellie's things for you. I know whom she'd want to have what, d'you see."

He did tell Ursula, but that was different; that was like talking to another, new, part of himself.

The call from Peggy Earl was a startling reminder that there was an everyday world, and that he was about to go back and live in it. He was reminded by her that he had a sitting in the studio at three o'clock, Artistry perfume, when could she expect him? And how long was Lukie to be a room-and-boarder?

"She's not a nuisance. Not all the time. She's thinking now she'll be a photographer. When not hanging on my every word and deed, she's in the darkroom, with Jim. Who"—pointedly—"is engaged. I thought engagements were out. Not with Lotus Quinn, they aren't."

"Just hang on until the smoke clears, Peg, and that should be soon."

Almost on cue, Berenson called him and said, "Talk about anti-climaxes. Tost was being booked at seven thirty this morning at the Fourteenth Precinct. You'd think he'd have planned a little change of pace in jail, something new. But, armed robbery again. A furrier's on Fifty-seventh Street. Just a kind of hiccup, this call. They'll be bringing him down to see me a bit later, but from what you told Calder he's beside the point."

In a dimmed crimson one-room apartment on erratically an-gling West Fourth Street two blocks northwest of Timothy, an unseen curtain was going up.

Hildegarde Lasalle, otherwise known to the Village as the Lady in Red, woke up feeling able to cope for the first time since Monday morning.

A touch of bronchitis, she had termed it. Surely it had nothing to do with the horrible death of that nice woman—Miss Legg? Head? Hand?—which she had heard, or overheard, about Sun-day night while sipping her Pernod at Rick's.

So much younger than she was, actually when you thought about it a comparatively *young* woman, certainly not near her sixties. So doughty, cheerful, living alone and thriving on it. Until—

There was a light knock on her door at eight thirty. It was her neighbor from down the hall, Mr. Bonsinger—elderly, courtly, a retired watchmaker, his first name never offered or asked for— come to inquire about her health, and carrying a little tray with two cups of hot chocolate on it, and a newspaper, the *Villager*.

"I thought you might be able to take a little nourishment," he said. They were old friends; he had been most kind, the past few days, bringing her hot soup and tea and urging aspirin upon her. "But nothing stronger. I fear and dread antibiotics, they sap one so."

She had gotten as far as getting up, making her bed, and wrap-ping herself in her red wool robe. They sat cozily on the shabby old loveseat, sipping chocolate, discussing the weather possibilities. She had no radio to give her a report; a radio brought the world in with it. She was accustomed to parting the heavy red velvet curtains each morning and doing her own forecasting.

"A little ad in the personals," Mr. Bonsinger said, reaching for the paper. "I thought you might be interested. She was so nice. Or, if I gather the import correctly, she is *still* so nice."

He gave Hildegarde the paper with its turned-back page. "Nellie lives. J.O. 20 Timothy Street."

"But how . . . marvelous." Slow astonished voice. "Then it was all gossip and distortion. D'you think though that it's true?"

"Let us hope so. I'll leave the paper with you, shall I?"

She had no telephone. The worst news of her life had come to her over the phone, the death of the man she loved, the man who loved her in red.

She washed the chocolate cups, bathed, did her hair and face, and looked restlessly about her silent room. Normally at this hour she would read her Yeats, or Emily Dickinson, or her *New Oxford Book of English Verse*.

But she knew she wouldn't be able to concentrate. There was no point in driving herself crazy, wondering. It was a pleasant day, sunny. It would surprise Mr. Bonsinger to be served flaky hot croissants with his breakfast tomorrow. They had very good croissants at the bakery just around the corner from Timothy Street.

It would do her good, make life seem less uncertain, hazardous, hung about with doom, to look again on that nice woman's cheerful face.

"Don't leave me," Jeremy said to Ursula as he pressed the buzzer button for Enid. "I need you for moral support and every other kind of support known to man."

"I hope you're prepared to be grilled. Enid prides herself on knowing everything there is to be known about what goes on in the Village."

"Interrupt me with some female irrelevancy if you feel I'm being backed into a corner. Such as, dear Jeremy, I do love you." He went to the door and opened it to Enid.

"Those stairs," Enid gasped. "Although Nellie went up them like a gazelle. It's supposed to be better for your heart climbing stairs than it is going down them, but I wonder when it *stops* being good for your heart?"

Busy, prepared chatter; not like her. She looked ill and tired, eyes too bright over color-patched cheekbones. But elegant in her old black Norell.

"Hello, Ursula. Yes, I will take coffee, and whatever you have to offer, in it. I haven't quite got it through my head yet. *Matthew!* With, now, everything in the world to live for."

Jeremy poured a generous tot of the remaining scotch into her coffee. She drank it, and said, "I haven't had a cigarette for five days. I think I'll have one now. Nellie keeps a pack for friends in the silver drawer. Will you bring it?"

Established in the slipper chair, she was taking charge of the room.

Cigarette lit for her by him, eyes on his face, raking, she said, "I'll say what neither of you has volunteered or perhaps even asked yourself yet. Could it be that Matthew had something to do with Nellie's death? And his—killing himself, here of all places, some kind of expiation? There are, after all"—she paused to draw on her cigarette and then with distaste ground it out on her saucer—"much taller buildings uptown. Rack my brains ever so hard, I can't see any *other* possible if mad explanation."

"By 'something to do with,' Enid, you mean that he killed her?" Jeremy asked.

"Oh, flat out like that, horrible. But still, why here? Unless, oh God, this sounds ridiculous, a last visit to the scene, and then overcome by it. Because I still feel Nellie here, don't you?" She looked searchingly around in a way Ursula found unnerving, as though Nellie at any minute would emerge from the kitchen or the bedroom.

"But . . . he couldn't have stopped here, because he'd have found you in residence. If you were in, that is, last night."

Enid's eyes, Jeremy felt, were piercing right through the bone of his forehead and into his brain.

"In and out," he said casually and truthfully. Down to Basil's for whom forever thank God, to arrange the borrowing of a cup of sugar.

There was a light tentative knock on the door, not the peremptory police knuckles Jeremy had been expecting.

The Lady in Red drew back a step when she saw him in the doorway. "Oh, I'm sorry, I didn't know that there was anyone else here, I just came to—"

She had been pointed out once to him by Nellie.

"Do come in." He felt her shyness, her obvious fear of being an unwanted intruder.

The Lady in Red advanced hesitantly until she stood just inside the living room. She was further daunted by Ursula, on the sofa, and Enid in her chair, but to balance this was encouraged by the look of a pleasant morning coffee party, nothing to do with death and mourning.

To Enid, whom she knew well by sight, she asked, "Is Miss— Is she here?"

"No," Jeremy said gently. "Did you expect her to be?"

"Yes, that notice in the paper, that she's alive, such a relief. I do apologize for bothering you but I just did want to see her and make sure. And then turn around and go."

She looked at Enid, memory almost visibly jogged. "But you'd know, of course, that she was perfectly all right at the time they said she was supposed to be—" Not liking the word dead, she left it in the air.

"I beg your pardon?" Enid's voice combined tolerance and impatience.

"I'd forgotten till now. It was seeing you here that reminded me. I do tend to forget things."

Eggshell-treading, Jeremy asked, "What things?"

"It was, yes, Saturday night. I'd been out late, to a very old friend's and I was walking home, frightening but then she's only three blocks from me. I saw Miss—" groping unsuccessfully for the name.

"Callender," Enid said with recovered patience.

"Miss Callender coming out of the door here. It was a few minutes after midnight. I'd left my friend's on the dot of twelve. I thought it would be a comfort to keep reasonably close behind her on the street, company of a kind. She was—you were carrying a small television set. And then you put it into one of those big wire trash baskets."

She was eager now, as if to show that when she put her mind to it she could produce perfect clarity of observation. "I thought about the set and in the morning I told Mr. Bonsinger—my neighbor—that it might still be there. He cannot afford one. By some chance it *was* still there, all but buried at the bottom. He was most pleased. It works beautifully, he says. He's already spending a great deal of time watching it. I do not have a set of my own and"—now feeling something in the atmosphere about her, something strange, frightening, she finished hurriedly—"do not desire one. The world is too much with us late and soon. Is that perhaps St. Paul?"

A bus accelerated on Sixth Avenue, two short blocks east. George's claws could be heard on the scratching post in the kitchen. A breeze lifted Nellie's blue-and-white gingham cafe curtain and then let it float back into place.

"But I fear I am disturbing you. Will you tell her when she comes back that I inquired for her? And am so glad, so happy, that it was all a false alarm."

The Lady in Red left with an antique and impressive grace, closing the door quietly behind her.

"Poor thing," Enid murmured. "Poor thing. Of course she's quite mad. But so unfair to delude her—do you wonder, Jeremy, that I was so angry about that abominable notice of yours?"

"There is, though," Jeremy said, a curious reluctance in his voice, "the portable television set, which as you remember was among the items stolen."

He leaned forward, on the sofa, hands loosely locked between his knees, eyes vivid and very dark. "The set may be a delusion too, and Mr. Bonsinger—but that's just a brief matter of checking. I suppose the serial number of the Sony would be on the warranty card she'd have mailed in as a matter of course."

Enid bent down for her handbag and her crewel-embroidered shopping bag. She got up slowly, as though her bones were aching. Jeremy got up too and stood looking into the eagle face. He felt a gush of sadness; like watching a wrecking ball swing slowly toward a fine old town house about to be powdered into flying masonry and glass and wood and dust.

"You already have one murderer for your aunt, Jeremy," Enid said, blazingly meeting his eyes. "Do you require two?"

"I'm sorry, Enid." Peculiar thing to say; it came out without his thinking about his answer.

A swift motion involving the shopping bag, and then a little gun appeared in Enid's bony and slightly shaking hand. Ursula had risen to stand beside Jeremy. He put an arm across her body.

"I've carried this ever since Lukie's little trouble. I intend no harm with it to anybody unless necessary—only self-protection. Jeremy, you will stay where you are. Ursula, you will please come with me as my escort, down the stairs, and get me a cab. I will be right beside you with this, and as I say I would much prefer not to use it."

A picture came fleetingly back to him, the photograph over the bed, Enid and her husband on a lion-hunting trip presumably in Africa. She would know how to use a gun. And a knife.

Her eyes went to the savage clenching of a fist at his side. He wanted to strike the gun upward from her hand, but it was too chancy. Ursula was too near.

"No, Jeremy, no. I gather there's some kind of tie now between you two. Just what Nellie wanted, wasn't it? It would be too bad to cut it off in its infancy."

Ursula's voice was quiet. "I'll go with Enid. I can't think of any reason why she should shoot me on the stairs or in the street."

"Well, only the one reason. Now you know, too," Enid said. Her reasonableness was more frightening than open aggression.

Ursula's eyes, which by now he could read very well, told him, begged him to obey.

"You directly in front of me, Ursula," Enid ordered. "I believe that's the classic manner of doing this sort of thing." A loop of the embroidered bag hung over her forearm, hand deep in the bag, hand on the little gun.

One flight, two, Jeremy standing in the doorway, looking down, frozen. At any second some final desperate panic might seize Enid.

It is all over and nothing matters now.

Useless to think of following them, however silently. She might turn and look back and up. He had never in his life felt so ragingly helpless.

Ursula's burnished head was lost from sight. He thought he heard a sound of footsteps coming up from below.

Berenson passed the two women on the second landing. "Good morning," he said politely, feeling one of them was somehow familiar. Oh yes, the red-haired girl who had found Nellie Hand's body; he remembered the description in the report.

Ursula had no idea who he was but to maintain an air of normality which might very possibly mean her life gave him back a good morning.

They were two steps from the front hall when Berenson came into Jeremy's view. Voice low, words tumbling over each other, Jeremy said, "Just now on the stairs, two women, the older one has a gun, you'll want her—you'd better stop her, get her, right away, but for Christ's sake—"

Berenson got his message. "Redhead's in the clear. Okay." He turned and ran lightly down the stairs, Jeremy close behind him. The Inspector went out the front door and moved to Ursula. She was signaling a cab for her elderly companion whose hand was buried in her shopping bag.

A cab drew up. The elderly woman got into it. Berenson caught the handle of the closing door and got in with her. Aided by her astonishment, he snatched the shopping bag off her wrist, saw the hand still holding the gun, and with the edge of his palm struck hard. The gun fell to the floor.

"What the hell is this?" the driver asked. "I don't want no carrying on and fighting and quarreling in my cab."

"Sixth Precinct, Tenth Street," Berenson said, and as the cab pulled away Ursula and Jeremy, on the curb, heard the pouring screams and, silenced to their cores, looked away from each other.

Then Jeremy said, "This is usually a bad street for cabs. We'd better go over to Sixth."

Temporarily beyond coherent thought, Ursula asked childishly, "Oh God, do we *have* to?"

"Yes." He took her hand. "We have to."

After an hour at the station house, during the first half of which Ursula and Jeremy made up a dreadful threesome with Enid, attended by Berenson and Sergeant Sundburg, Enid was formally charged with the murder of Nellie Hand.

She had recovered herself, or transposed herself into a figure of iron, tearless, unresisting, explicit; and sounding profoundly bored with having to fill in the blanks.

Her cousin Charles Lambert had ("unprofessionally, of course, but we're quite close") informed her several weeks before that Lise's long law battle for her money was about to be ended in her and her sister's favor. He also told her the sum of money involved. Lise's was by far the greater of the two shares: nine hundred thousand dollars.

"Well, d'you see, I'd been Lise's heir for years. Then we had a tiff about something, I forget what, didn't speak for a week, and she did that silly home-for-cats thing just to plague Gretel. And after a month decided on Nellie. I suppose in the long run she might have split it between us, but there's no possible way to be sure. And she *could* die at any time. Yesterday. Tomorrow."

She couldn't tell them, because she didn't know, exactly when she had made up her mind to do something about Nellie. "I knew of course as night follows day that if Nellie died I'd be automatically reinstated. We two of all the people in the world were by far the closest to her. She even told me once that if anything happened to Nellie I'd be named again. She loves talking about her will, playing with it, as Nellie used to say, but I know her, I know her basic loyalties."

With robberies and crime flourishing all about them—"Actually it was the affair of my niece's apartment that lit the match, so to speak"—she had proceeded with her project and then set her stage.

"That damned television set. But they *always* take television sets. It wasn't three minutes after I went out the door that I got rid of it, or thought I had. No, officer, I am not going to slip a poison capsule under my tongue. I am merely fumbling for the pack of cigarettes provided for me by Nellie to assist at this extremely trying time."

As if speaking to herself, she added in a kind of summing up, "Things weren't going well at Babylon, and worse was in sight. To go over the brink from elderly to old, broke, perhaps ill, when instead I could live with a little grace, a little dignity—or no, correct that, a lot of both."

She waved her cigarette impatiently. "I won't continue to bore you. I have nothing else to say."

Half a block from the station house, Ursula asked in a color-less voice, "But what about Matthew?"

"I don't know. Maybe no one will ever know." He had been deciding, off and on in the grim little room with the five of them in it, that he would have a private talk with Berenson. And ask if there was any possibility that Matthew's attempt on his life could be kept permanently silent.

Matthew was dead. And Matthew had not killed Nellie. But the savage ugly story of the interval preceding his death would crash over his wife, across the news and across the nation. He supposed it would be an advantage, this silencing, to the police: a cleaner, simpler job, an everyday suicide, no face-to-face follow-ups against the corporate might of UBC.

Basil, he thought, would probably go along this discreet path with him; Basil would hardly want police busying themselves about his person and premises.

As they stood at the corner of Tenth Street and Fifth Avenue, Ursula said desolately, "I have the most peculiar feeling of home-lessness, and not belonging anywhere. I don't want to go back to Timothy Street right now, and you're due I gather at your studio."

A wedding party emerged from Trinity Church across the street: color and gaiety, morning clothes and white veiling and breezes of confetti.

Jeremy looked at her drawn face, bonier than it should be. "You're coming with me. I thought you'd taken that for granted. We'll try to do something to put both of us together again."